THE ARCHER AND THE PRINCE

EMMA STEINBRECHER

Contents

FAIRVEIN TIMELINE

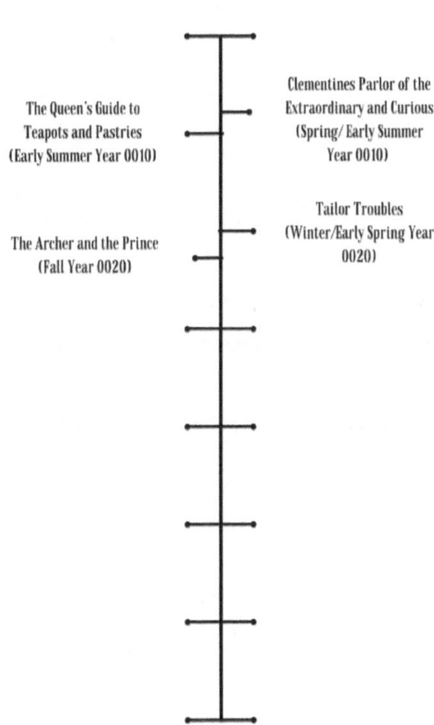

FOREWORD

As Monroe and I continue to explore the magical world of Fairvein, we are giving stories to the many characters we have already created and will create in the future.

The male love interest in this story, Tobias, is a man of color. He is written and depicted in art as black.

Since I am a white writer, I knew it would be important to self-reflect, research, and take other important steps before publishing this novella.

This story has been combed through by a paid sensitivity reader for anything that may perpetuate any harmful stereotypes. However, if you read this and find something that doesn't sit right with you or something that was missed, please don't hesitate to reach out to me via email.

esteinbrauthor@gmail.com

To Dad

I would know next to nothing about archery without you.

Love you

PROLOGUE

"Don't you dare!"

I watched as Woodrow sprinted across the grassy field, barefoot and covered in dirt. Reaching down, I grabbed the hem of my skirt, dirty from its time dragging over the soil, and tied a firm knot to hold it above my kneecaps.

"Luna!" Nassanine placed her hands on her knees, catching her breath as I grinned over my shoulder. "What are you doing?"

I waved my slingshot at her, the grin still fixed on my face. "I'm going to teach Woodrow a lesson." I picked up my ammunition as Nassanine scanned me from the top of my red hair, over the tied-up skirt, and down to my muddy boots.

"And what lesson is that? Also, how many petticoats are you wearing?"

"None." I kept my eyes fixed on Woodrow's back as he sank down between the grass and flowers. *What a fool.* "And I'm teaching him that I'm faster and smarter."

Nassanine scoffed, but I could hear the slight smile despite her desire to hide it.

Launching myself into a full sprint, I relished in the summer wind whipping through my hair. The scent of aline berries and mud swirled with the breeze. When I neared Woodrow, he shot up, his pointed ears sticking out from the brown mop of hair he'd grown to his shoulders.

"Any last words?" I asked, lifting my slingshot and loading my ammunition.

Woodrow's eyes were wide and pitch black, as if his hazel irises had been swallowed by his fear.

"I thought we were friends." His voice came out as a whimper, and I launched my attack.

The aline berry hit the elf right above his eye, painting his pale complexion with the deep pink juice. I popped one in my mouth, laughing at his shocked expression.

He wiped the remains of the berry from his face, shaking his hand as his scowl deepened. "I thought you were loading rocks into that thing!"

A laugh ripped from deep in my belly as Nassanine strode up beside me. Her strands of black hair flew around her face, decorating her grin like the ribbons my father used every winter solstice.

"Thirteen or not, I'd never use real stones, Woodrow. I'm not that naive."

The bell tower tolled, and Woodrow looked up at the sky, still streaked orange from today's sun. "I have to go," he stated. "Mother will be wondering where I am. I've got evening chores, you know."

I waved a hand. "Yes, yes. The farmer's son. We know." Woodrow's mother and father had traveled to Fairvein from the continent. While the island of Fairvein provided a slower pace, fully funded by the summer tourism each year, those on the continent found our little island to be full of silly and incompetent people. They believed us to be inferior and lacking the work ethic of those across the water.

Nobody on the continent seemed to mind my father, though. As the general of the royal's army, he did well for himself, though he was often gone. They didn't find *him* silly at all.

It proved their prejudice incorrect.

Woodrow sprinted through the grass, clearly late for whatever chores awaited him as I threw myself down, staring up at the sky dotted with plush white clouds.

Nassanine joined me, straightening her skirt before giving up on her cleanliness and laying down properly.

"Aline berry?" I asked, holding out the last of my ammunition.

Nassanine took one and popped it into her mouth before talking around the sweet fruit. "You have to be careful with these," she said. "I heard they can sometimes encourage feelings of infatuation."

I scoffed. "Oh please. I am fully capable of infatuation on my own."

She giggled, snatching another one out of my hand. "Do tell, Luna. Who is it you are infatuated with?"

I drummed my fingers on my stomach, keeping my eyes firmly fixed to the floating clouds above. "Woodrow?" I supplied, though my voice came out a question.

Nessanine sat up on her elbow, completely aghast. "No, you are not!"

I peeked over at her, smiling at the way her mouth hung open, tongue and teeth painted pink from the berries. "Not really," I admitted. Though Woodrow and I had been friends since he moved to Fairvein, I had never considered him as more. "Plus," I added, "I'm not even sure he likes girls."

Nessanine threw herself back down in the grass, joining me in staring up at the sky. "You're probably right."

"Do you think it matters?" I questioned. "I do happen to prefer pants."

"You are improper," she scolded. Nassanine's parents were also from the continent and friends with my father. They often vacationed in Fairvein for the summer season, though I always found them a bit too starched for my liking. Nassanine pretended to be like that, but I knew deep down she had a free spirit, something inside her that longed to run through fields with other elven children as they launched berries at one another.

"I guess there is someone I fancy." My voice lowered as if I were hesitantly sharing a grand secret. And I supposed I was. But there were none greater to share secrets with than one's closest friends.

"Tell me," she demanded.

"Have you seen the prince?" I asked. Prince Tobias Cranefield was nearly fifteen, two years my senior, and beyond charming. I'd only heard stories of the prince from my father, but he always seemed to be up to something–sneaking from the palace to participate in midnight swims or releasing fire sprites during his parents' important dinners.

Any boy who did that clearly had a sense of humor. Not to mention how handsome he was.

"I have seen him," Nassanine admitted. "But, Luna! He's the prince!"

I giggled, stretching my arms out and placing my hands behind the back of my head in the grass. "Yes, and I should like to kiss him."

Nessanine laughed so fiercely a wild sound shot out of her nose and through the field. It sounded like one of the boars on Woodrow's farm and made me join in the laughter, too.

"See, now," I began as my laughter subsided. "I should not like to kiss Woodrow, but the prince seems nice."

Silence stretched between us as we listened to the birds chirp from the trees off in the distance. The woods surrounding Fairvein held mysteries I didn't dare try to solve. It was said a witch lived beyond the treeline–a dangerous woman who often turned humans and elves, like myself, into toads.

The sound of armor clinking drew my attention, and I shot to my feet, watching as my father urged his horse through the grass, his eyes wild as he searched the grounds for me. My stomach twisted at the sight. Something seemed amiss, especially when he stopped before us, his brows furrowing into a scowl I'd never seen my father make before.

"Luna," his voice boomed over the field, sending the distant birds alight. He quickly glanced behind him, and panic took hold of my chest. Something was certainly wrong. "You need to head home to your mother," he said, his tone strained. "I should be back later this evening."

I glanced at Nessanine, who held herself straight in the presence of the King and Queen's general. She didn't dare look at me, but I longed for her eyes to meet mine—to remind me that I wasn't alone.

Normally, I would argue. Beg for more time with friends, but something told me that wouldn't be happening.

I nodded once, fleeing across the field with Nessanine on my heels. My father didn't follow, but when I glanced back, I saw more horses cresting over the hill beyond, my father taking the opportunity to look back.

Averting my eyes, I pressed onward, though I swore I saw a tear tracking down his cheek, settling in the red beard my mother always asked him to be rid of.

It wasn't until later that evening, though, that I had become truly worried—even more so as the weeks passed and turned into months. News from the palace reached Fairvein, and I remember standing at a cart in town, fighting the tears leaking from my eyes—the betrayal I felt so deeply, I thought it would drown me like the sirens lurking in the water beyond the island.

My father had gone against the royals and had been executed for treason.

The final flame of hope winked out inside me, darkening my inner world and cooling my heart until it was nothing but stone beneath flesh.

As it turned out, my father had lied. He was never coming home.

ONE

If there was anything I'd learned in my twenty-six years of life, it was that a woman could solve any problem or puzzle so long as she was provided with a good pair of trousers. And even without them, her chances of success were quite good.

I trekked up the hill, passing the numerous shops decorating the island of Fairvein and dodging the tourists milling in the streets. The orange sun hung high above, complementing the auburn, red, and gold colors of the newly changed leaves. Since the summer season was coming to a close, it meant that autumn had descended on all of Edessa and that the final archery tournament for the year was set to take place in a few short days.

It also meant I was in desperate need of a new pair of trousers.

The autumn chill caught my hair as I stood before Birdie's Needle, the tailor's shop, a beacon of hope considering my favorite pair of pants had worn so thoroughly at the knee that I needed to find a replacement before leaving for the continent tomorrow.

Tucking the wild strand of red hair behind my pointed ear, I opened the door to the shop, hoping that the owner would be able to help me on such short notice. I couldn't stand the idea of competing in the championship archery tournament wearing a gown. It simply wouldn't do.

How was I to solve problems or puzzles?

"I'll be right with you."

I heard the voice float through the room from the back of the shop before my attention caught Isla sitting perched on a pink velvet couch against the wall to my left.

"Luna," she said, getting up and wrapping me in a warm embrace, and I stiffened. "I hope you don't mind the hug. I'm not in the tea shop, so professionalism is certainly unnecessary."

I chuckled as she pulled away. "When were you ever a stickler for professionalism, Isla?" I offered her a wide smile despite my discomfort. "It's part of what makes your tea shop so welcoming and successful."

"That's what I keep telling Cyris!" she said, the humor never leaving her green eyes.

Isla owned the tea shop on the island—the shop right across from Cyris's bakery. While I spent most of the summer traveling to the continent for archery competitions, something I preferred during the busy tourist season, I still made sure to stop at Isla's Teas and Treats whenever possible. As a former healer, the woman knew her way around herbs, and ever since Cyris helped her with her scone recipe, those had improved exponentially, too.

"No, it has to be extravagant, Birdie. A girl only gets this opportunity once in a lifetime!" Clementine appeared from the back of the store, her purple gown decorated with elegant embroidered flowers. Birdie, the tailor, followed closely behind with a handful of equally extravagant dresses, and I started to believe that I was the only creature on the island who appreciated the value of a good pair of pants.

"Clementine, it is a date with Cyris. Stop stressing the poor woman." Isla rolled her eyes, throwing herself onto the pink couch as Birdie passed the handful of gowns into Clementine's arms.

Clementine blinked a few times, her brown skin glowing in the warm light of the shop. After a long moment, her lush lips pulled into a full smile. "Of course. It's just a date," she answered. "You're still trying on every last one of these, though."

I chuckled, turning away to run my fingers over the glass case filled with jewelry as I awaited the tailor's attention. I wasn't sure if Birdie would be able to get me what I needed in time, but it was worth a shot. I surely wasn't going to borrow a pair of trousers from Woodrow before leaving. Besides, his trousers wouldn't be nearly long enough.

Birdie sidled up to me, her white, tea-length gown puffing out at the bottom and decorated with a delicate pink floral pattern that said she hadn't given up on the warm weather just yet. "Can I help you?" she asked, her muddy blonde hair falling across one shoulder in gentle waves.

"Yes," I responded, offering her a wide smile in return. "I was hoping to get a new pair of trousers made since I have Edessa's archery championship coming up. While I love dresses, I don't enjoy wearing them for competitions, you see."

Birdie clapped her hands together in excitement, her face brightening. "Yes, of course!" she said. "When do you need them, next week? I'd be happy to make as many pairs of pants as you need. If you enjoy the dresses too, I could sketch a few designs for those as well. Possibly combine the two." She tapped her chin, making her way across the dark wood floors and rounding the counter to pull out a sketchbook and a quill pen from the shelf. "We could design a gown with trousers underneath. Though, they'd come at an extra cost, of course. I could have these drawings ready for book club this week."

She looked up from the sketchbook—waiting. Her quill hovered over the parchment as if she were eager to begin the expensive design–her brown eyes hungry.

I'd spent a lot of time at book club in recent months. Maxwell's bookstore provided the perfect meeting spot, the books were always entertaining and exceptionally filthy, and I found the company enjoyable—if only in small doses.

Maybe I'd gotten used to the continent.

"That won't be necessary," I said. "Could you have them ready by tomorrow?"

"Tomorrow!" Her voice cracked on the word, pitching up an octave before she remembered herself, running her hands over the skirts of her dress. "Tomorrow, yes. Not an extravagant design. I'm wondering if I could take the trousers I already have made and adjust them for you. How many would you like? Two pairs? Five pairs?"

"Not five," I said, my eyes wide. "Two should be plenty."

"Only two?" she asked, one brow quirking upward as if she were challenging me.

My eyes narrowed. I'd heard rumors about Birdie from Maxwell up the way. Maxwell owned the bookshop, and he had warned me about Birdie's affinity for overselling her products in an attempt to get her customers to purchase more than they needed.

Though, it didn't stop them from meeting regularly after hours.

I liked to think they were playing cards, though I was certain that wasn't the truth.

The door chime rang, but I kept my eyes fixed firmly on the shop owner in front of me. She glanced behind me, her eyes widening before she cleared her throat.

"Why don't you wait on one of the couches while I gather this next order," she began, "and I'll take your measurements after. I should be able to get two pairs of trousers ready for tomorrow morning, though I'm afraid it'll cost more for the rush." Her smile widened—clearly satisfied with the upcharge. I decided it was deserved.

"Of course," I said with a polite smile of my own before turning and running right into the customer who'd just arrived. "Excuse me," I muttered, stumbling back a step.

"Not to worry." The man's deep voice sent a strange sensation down my spine, goosebumps forming on my arms. When I looked up to find dark eyes, a full mouth, and an utterly amused expression, I swallowed. "It's always a pleasure to run into a beautiful woman."

My gaze narrowed in suspicion at the casual flirtation rolling off the handsome stranger's tongue. Any man with enough charm to disarm a woman like that certainly held some fatal flaw, and while I stood there trying to piece together what his might be, I found myself coming up short.

No matter. By the man's accent alone, I could tell he came from the continent. A tourist, then.

"Do you make it a habit of running into beautiful women?" I challenged, his warm brown skin highlighted by the lights of the shop. "Do they usually swoon when you use that line?"

A deep laugh dragged from his lips, one that started low in his belly, I was certain. And while I attempted to hold my ground, I couldn't deny the way the sound made me want to lean in—the way it begged me to listen to every word he said.

"Women typically swoon, yes," he finally answered—confident as ever.

I felt the smirk pull at the corner of my mouth, satisfied that I had solved the puzzle so easily. The man's fatal flaw was that he was arrogant. And I didn't even have to wear my new trousers to figure it out.

"Well, I am sorry to disappoint," I said, promptly shoving past the handsome stranger and moving toward a gaping Isla and Clementine, who stood in the center of the floor.

While I didn't understand their shocked expressions or why the shop had grown so silent, I did understand the warm sensation rising to my cheeks. And despite my best efforts to hide it, I couldn't deny the impression the stranger had left on me with that small interaction.

Arrogant, yes. Charming?

Absolutely.

Two

"Explain to me, Luna, why you have showed up at my farmhouse well into the evening with a deep flush to your cheeks."

"Excuse me?" I stared at Woodrow, noting the way he stood with one hand firmly placed at his hip, his hair, now darker than it was when we were kids, tied up into a bun at the base of his skull.

"You heard me."

I rolled my eyes, shoving past him and prowling into the warm kitchen. The rough butcher block, worn with use, and gentle candles and lanterns flickering over the deep green cabinets reminded me why I spent so much time here. Woodrow's house was the only place I didn't feel I had to pretend–the last piece of home after losing my father.

Those on the continent found the inhabitants of Fairvein to be silly and naive. And while I hated to admit it, I found some of those sentiments to be true. My time in town was often spent smiling and accepting hugs I didn't long to receive because nobody in town knew of my past–they couldn't. Anything other than joy and optimism would draw attention in Fairvein and would surely raise suspicions.

Birdie, the tailor, had moved to the island with a somewhat mysterious past, and that had cost her reputation tremendously. Maxwell hated the woman–convinced she was out to swindle all of the inhabitants. I couldn't imagine how I'd be treated should the town connect me with the thirteen-year-old elven girl whose father betrayed the crown.

Woodrow knew of my past, though. And so, I found comfort in the home where I'd whispered many of my secrets. I'd detailed the execution of my father to Woodrow–explained how I'd seen him in the field that same day and been told to run home. I recounted moving to the continent because of my mother's desire to start over. I cried when I had returned, feeling the warm embrace of Woodrow's farmhouse. I had wandered back here, realizing that maybe there was something in my spirit that hadn't settled on the continent–hadn't accepted my father's decisions.

Woodrow hummed as he grabbed a jar of herbs for tea from the shelf above the sink. The tune unfamiliar to me.

"You're doing it again." Woodrow tossed a wan smile over his shoulder before grabbing a thick mug and placing it on the counter.

I tracked his movements, shaking the memories from my brain. It was easy to keep them at bay in town while I pretended. Much harder in the places I felt safe.

"Doing what?" I asked.

"You're lost in thought again." Woodrow pulled a kettle from the hearth and prepared a cup of tea. He was no Isla, but it would do. "You seem to be thinking of something morose. It's a stark contrast from the way you looked when you arrived, and trust me, I have not forgotten."

I looked down at the hot liquid in my cup, forcing myself to take a drink and hide the reddening of my cheeks. If he had caught even a hint of interest in my expression, he would not settle until all the details were spilled on the ground.

Woodrow leaned on the kitchen island, propping his head in his hand. "Tell me," he began, "Was he handsome?"

I rolled my tongue along my cheek, refusing to answer despite knowing my dearest friend could read me like a book. His interest in my love life was far too involved, considering I had no love life to speak of.

He gasped, slapping the wooden countertop and causing me to jolt. "He was! Please tell me he's from the continent. If you've gotten romantic feelings for someone I grew up with, I will vomit. Cyris has already been taken. Same as Maxwell. I fear there are very few handsome men of an appropriate age left on the island for you."

I smiled, shaking my head and bringing the mug to my lips again. "Nonsense," I said. "You're here."

"It would be unfortunate if you fell in love with me," Woodrow admitted. "I am already in love with the man who made that mug you're drinking out of."

My eyes widened. "The potter up the hill?" I set the mug down, failing to keep its contents contained. "You're serious!"

Woodrow tapped a finger on the counter, a smug smirk painting his lips. "Now, Luna. I've told you my secrets. You tell me yours."

I rolled my eyes. "We are not children."

"By elven standards, we are quite young. Now, out with it!"

My face fell as my brows furrowed, and I gripped the mug tighter. Woodrow knew as well as anyone why I couldn't pursue a romantic relationship with anyone, yet he sometimes needed the reminder. "Just some stranger from Birdie's shop," I replied, keeping my eyes fixed to the liquid in my cup. "You know why it could never be anything more."

"That's ridiculous."

I finally looked up, hazel eyes blazing. "Woodrow, if I got romantically involved with someone, it would ruin everything. I can't imagine a relationship without trust, and I'd be lying to them from the begin-ning—lying about who I am."

"Or," he began, turning to grab a damp cloth and wipe down the counter. "You could tell them the truth."

THREE

Even though I'd made the trip hundreds of times, I was always nervous on the ferry ride over to Fairtree. Something about the rocking waves, the tourists packed on the boat, and the sirens that lurked in the water below made my stomach churn. This time was no different.

I'd picked up my new trousers early in the morning, packing my bag with various gowns, trousers, and blouses that were a delicate balance between tight but also flexible for the purpose of the archery competitions. My stomach rocked with the waves tossing the ferry as a few dozen tourists gathered around, and I fought the urge to expel the contents of my stomach.

It would be a pity, really, considering I had eaten an early breakfast at Cyris's bakery. While the cinnamon and apple puffed pastries tasted delightful on the way down, I wasn't sure they'd have the same effect coming back up.

Clutching my bag tightly to my chest, I slid to the end of the bench on the ferry, resting my head on its back and closing my eyes. Pink sunlight warmed my pale skin, and I was suddenly thankful for the herbal lotion Isla had gifted me. I didn't want to burn, especially not so early on in my trip.

The boat rocked, and my face twisted against the slow rise of hours-old pastry desperately trying to make its appearance as a shadow hovered over me.

"I wouldn't have taken you for an elf, nor any other creature, who would suffer from sea sickness."

That voice–

My eyes popped open to see a silhouette backed by the hanging sun standing in front of me. The man, who I quickly recalled on account of his handsome appearance and deep voice, stood with his hands clasped behind his back. The first few buttons on his white linen shirt were undone; his sleeves rolled up his forearms as he stared down at me with an unwarranted intensity that made my skin feel hot and flushed all at the same time.

I was used to arrogant men, especially being from Fairvein. I spent enough time on the continent to know that its inhabitants thought those from the island were simple, silly creatures. Even so, this type of arrogance seemed to disarm me. Maybe it was the chiseled jawline, the dark cropped hair, or maybe, and it was a big maybe, it was the fact those from the continent were quite right, and I was simply stupid.

"Are you insulting me?" I asked, keeping my head back on the bench, refusing to move on account of the nausea I still felt.

He took a deep breath, his hands still clasped firmly behind him. "I've met you twice now, so I happen to consider us dear friends. Friends occasionally insult one another in jest, do they not?"

The *stranger* licked his lips, suppressing a smile that threatened to break free.

Despite myself, I huffed a laugh, joining him in concealing the gentle tug trying to pull at the corner of my mouth. "You sound exactly like someone who does not have very many friends."

He shifted, moving to sit next to me on the bench and causing that irritating heat to rise to my cheeks. I hoped he couldn't see it.

"You've proven my point," he said, stretching his long legs out in front of him. I quickly looked away. "We are friends, then."

"You do not even know my name," I said, my brows furrowed.

"Ah, but *you* know *mine*."

His smug smirk told me everything I needed to know. The man was arrogant enough to believe I would recognize him for some unknown reason. Was his ego honestly that inflated?

"No," I said, my tone flat. I settled into my seat, closing my eyes once more when the boat rocked. "I do not."

I didn't need to open my eyes to feel the subtle tension in the air or the way he shifted uncomfortably on the bench.

Still, I opened one eye and noted the confused twisting of his features–the way he struggled to process the fact that I hadn't recognized him or heard of him for whatever reason.

"I know you're from the tailor's shop," I began, "but I do not find myself lying awake at night haunted by the memory of charming strangers."

He rolled his tongue along his cheek, dark eyes sliding over to me and lighted with amusement. I quickly closed my own eyes again to avoid his gaze. "You find me charming?" he asked.

"I find you somewhat irritating," I answered. "I thought I'd be able to sleep on this ride over to Fairtree, but as it turns out, I am being harassed by my dearest and closest friend–" I paused, cracking my eyelids open and allowing myself to observe him with careful scrutiny. I settled on a name that seemed fitting. "Albert."

"Albert?" he questioned, that confused expression returning.

"You look like an Albert," I supplied. The conversation had taken my mind off my growing nausea, and I found myself feeling significantly better. I put my leather bag on the ground, pulling the case where I kept my bow from beneath the seat. Picking up my bag and my bow, I nodded once to *Albert*, offering him a wide smile. "If you'll excuse me," I said before turning to flee.

Walking to the other end of the Ferry and listening to the tourists gush about the stores and activities, I found myself fighting the urge to smile. It wouldn't be a casual smile or a content smile, but a giddy smile. The kind of smile girls often held when they had obsessive crushes on the young boys in their neighborhood. It was the kind of grin accompanied by sketches of hearts and initials and daydreams.

It was the kind of smile that, quite frankly, aggravated me.

I didn't have time for silly crushes or hearts on parchment. I needed to focus on getting to Draymore for the championship.

If I had any hope of getting noticed by the royals—any hope of being put on the royal guard on account of my talents, this would be the time for such an endeavor. It was the first championship hosted in the same city as the palace, and while I'd earned a name for myself over the past few years, a name wouldn't do anything for my hopes of joining the royal guard.

No, *Albert* and his distractions wouldn't do.

So, after I found my way to the opposite end of the ferry, I kept my gaze firmly fixed on the water, watching the blue waves glitter beneath the pink light of the sun and forcing myself to think about the one and only thing I'd been born to do—archery.

FOUR

The journey to Draymore had been uneventful, and hopelessly long.

Upon arriving in Fairtree, I made it my one and only goal to avoid *Albert,* or whatever his true name happened to be. I quickly grabbed my things, fled the ferry, and found my way to the livery stable to rent myself a horse for the journey.

They'd given me a gelding named Dominion, and while the name was incredibly intimidating, the horse's temperament was decidedly not. He was sweet, docile, afraid of bumblebees, and had an affinity for apples. I decided to call him Minion instead since he was so compliant. I wasn't sure if it was rude to the horse. While I was elven, I was no elven guard–not bonded to the creature–so I hadn't the slightest idea if he found it offensive. It did make me laugh, and he hadn't thrown me throughout the journey, so I assumed it was all right.

Upon arriving in Draymore, I quickly returned my horse to the local livery and walked my way through the crowded streets to a nearby inn.

Draymore reminded me of Fairvein, but somehow less lively, less fun, and less like home. While half-timbered buildings, and narrow cobbled streets lined with black streetlamps decorated the city, the people weren't quite as warm. I was used to the attitudes on the continent, but something about Draymore felt as if everyone believed they were a good deal more important than everyone.

I kept my gaze forward, listening to the sounds of carriage wheels rolling over stones and busy market vendors anxious to make money—and willing to swindle people to do it.

Opening the door to The Nuxberry Inn, I found my way to the bar, ordering a large bowl of soup and practically salivating at the idea of eating something other than food on horseback.

As soon as my vegetable stew was delivered, I settled into the routine of returning to the continent. My mind spun in circles, trying to concoct the best strategy to win the competition. Draymore was the city that housed the royal palace. If I were to be noticed for my skill, it would be here. And if I were to be noticed, I'd gain access to knowledge—knowledge that could guide me in understanding my father's decisions.

"Well, if it isn't the champion archer herself."

I dropped my spoon, splashing broth and cooked carrots onto the counter before I swiveled in my chair.

Nessanine's hair had been cut short to her shoulders, and she had swapped her prim gowns for a pair of trousers—perfect for archery competitions and solving problems, I noted.

I leapt from my seat, throwing my arms around her neck and nearly taking us both to the worn wooden floors below. Thankfully, she held strong. It would be a shame to fall into whatever sticky substance stuck to my shoes on my way in.

"Ness!" I laughed, squeezing her tighter until she made a fake coughing noise and pried me off her.

Nassanine couldn't hide her smile as she looked me over, eyes bright. "Looking well as ever, Lu."

I nervously ran my hands over my shirt to protect myself from taking the compliment. "So," I began. "Last you wrote, you had moved to Sevinton. How is the salty sea air treating you?"

"To be quite honest, not well." Her nose crinkled as if drawing up an unpleasant memory. "It smells of fish. *Always.*" She chuckled, tucking a short strand of hair behind her pointed ear. "I didn't realize that my apartment would be so close to the fish market–or that the smell would stretch on for miles."

"How unfortunate," I said with a saccharine smile.

Nassanine shoved at my shoulder, clearly not taking my false compassion. "Enough of that," she chided. "I've come to see you compete. I believe I mentioned the possibility in my last letter."

My heart warmed, my fingers itching to touch my bowstring. "Of course," I said. A twisting sensation formed in my stomach, one that churned like sour milk. There was more riding on this competition than the ones in the past, and while I'd made a name for myself, there was always a chance something could go wrong.

"I'm quite nervous," I admitted, already feeling my palms dampen.

Nessanine placed a gentle hand on my shoulder, leaning in with a devious smirk. "You know what would cure that?" she asked, her eyes flicking to the bar. "I say we drink."

My brows furrowed. "Do you think that's a good idea?"

She straightened, a smug expression overtaking her features. "Why," she began. "I think it's the very best idea I've ever had."

Somewhere in the back of my mind, I realized that drinking was not the very best idea ever had, but my alcohol-addled brain couldn't quite make sense of the matter. The evening felt stress-free, filled with laughter and a certain silliness I'd been missing since the day Nessanine last left Fairvein.

It reminded me of long summer days running through fields and hurling aline berries.

"Do you think him handsome?" Nassanine slurred, leaning toward me from where she sat at our table. I nearly toppled off the chair, and something about my lack of balance came across as extremely hilarious. In fact, everything was hilarious.

"I think him comical," I said as I laughed, a deep sound dragged from the very pit of my belly. "I suppose he *could* be handsome. Another drink will confirm it." I reached forward, grabbing a mug of ale. When I'd first tasted it, it had been bitter and horrible–a reminder that I'd never really liked beer to begin with. But with each sip, I found myself enjoying the taste–or possibly the fizzy feeling in my head.

I took another swig, thinking it the best drink I'd ever had. Possibly better than Isla's tea back on the island.

Ness slapped my shoulder just shy of too hard, and I giggled.

"That there!" she shouted. "The man walking through the door. Now *that* is a handsome man."

My eyes slid in the direction, and I giggled once more behind my cup. "Oh, him?" I said. "That's Albert. I met him on the ferry."

Albert had certainly changed his clothes and bathed. Something about his appearance and the memory of his casual charm sent heat to my already warmed cheeks.

"Oh!" Ness said, leaning sideways in her chair. "You *met* him." My eyes flicked to hers, catching her meaning.

"I did not sleep with him if that is what you're implying."

"But you should, Lu! That is the most beautiful man I've laid eyes on. Everyone in Sevinton smells like the fish market. He looks like he smells like–"

Nessanine paused, spending a longer time processing what she would say next than normal. It made me huff a laugh before pulling another sip from my mug.

"He looks like he smells like a good romp."

"Ness!" I screeched, tilting my head back and laughing. When I sat up and opened my eyes, that familiar stranger stood over our table, staring at me with a wide smile on his face, his hands folded behind his back.

"How are you?" he asked, something so genuine about the way he said it–the way his plush lips wrapped around the words he spoke. "No longer sick from the ferry?"

Nessanine burst out laughing. "We're drunk!" she shouted, her own drink sloshing over the lip of its container.

"I see that," he said. He seemed amused by the fact, but the expression was short-lived. His brows furrowed, concern wrinkling the spot between them. "Have you an escort?" he asked, glancing around the now-busy Inn.

"An escort?" I scoffed. "We are staying here."

"Ah," he mused, still taking in the scene around him. It seemed that the patrons stopped to stare at him, too. No doubt because he was so handsome. He probably did smell like a good romp.

"What was that?" he asked.

Under normal circumstances, I would have been embarrassed, but given my state, I could hardly find a reason to care. "You are very handsome," I said, pulling myself from my chair and stumbling into him. I couldn't help but notice the flex of his arm muscle where my hand had landed. I kept my gaze fixed there–mesmerized and thinking thoughts I ought not ponder.

"Okay," he said. "You are in no state to be in Draymore alone."

"Are you going to take advantage of me, Albert?"

Disgust painted his beautiful face, causing embarrassment to creep past my carefree demeanor. "Absolutely not," he said, his tone sharp like a blade.

I felt the room sway, my stomach sloshing with something unpleasant. My heart rate picked up, a fullness rising as my eyes widened. "I think–"

I didn't get to finish my words. The room swayed, my memories escaping me except for one last and final detail.

The only thing I could recall vividly was the sight of soiled shoes–far too nice to be sticking to the floor of a simple Inn.

FIVE

Mornings in Fairvein always came gently–the sunlight spilling through open windows like honey slowly dripping from its jar.

It was as if the sunshine knew to knock before it graced the island. Respectful. Kind.

Nothing like the harsh orange rays hitting me like a carriage descending a steep hill. I groaned, rolling over and covering my head with one of the plush Inn pillows.

In fact, it seemed that the Inn had provided a mound of pillows for my night's rest. It was far more than I could have ever hoped for, seeing that I was on a tight budget whenever I traveled for competitions.

The throbbing in my head refused to ease, and I finally decided I should drag myself into the land of the living by uncovering my face and taking in the assaulting sunrays.

When my eyes opened, I noted the large room–much too large for The Nuxberry Inn. The walls were painted a sea-foam green, lined with gold, and going on for miles upward to the vaulted ceiling. Large windows stood to my right–the source of the sunlight.

I blinked–trying to get my bearings–figure out where I was.

Nessanine and I had decided to enjoy all that the Inn's bar had to offer. We drank and laughed. I remembered talking loudly among the patrons. I could recall shoes covered in vomit.

I gasped, clasping my hand over my mouth. Albert–or whatever his name may be–had been at the tavern with us. I'd flirted with him.

Very poorly, I might add.

"Oh god," I whispered before looking down at the plush comforter, embroidered in gold with delicate floral patterns. The emerald shirt I wore did not belong to me. Its silk fabric felt snug around my chest until I realized the garment had been put on backward. I quickly corrected it as best I could without taking the thing off completely. The matching pajama bottoms were, thankfully, on correctly.

My feet hit the pristine white tile as I padded over to the door.

I don't know what I expected when I opened the door. The dread filling my stomach could be justified by a number of unpleasant guests or creatures.

The one thing I hadn't expected was Albert, fully clothed in white and gold–an outfit far too nice for anyone I'd ever encountered on the island of Fairvein.

Without hesitation, I opened the door fully, standing tall as I did. I know I was drunk the night before, and my memory after the shoes seemed to fail me, but there was no sense in cowering.

"Albert," I said, fighting the urge to brush my fingers over my hair to smooth down any stray strands.

"You're awake," he said, hands clasped behind his back as he did often. It was as if he'd been trained to stand in the position.

"I am," I asserted, mustering all the confidence I had. "I'd like to know the way back to the tavern. If you'd be so kind."

"Ah, yes." A ghost of a smile appeared on his lips. "Well, you may want to get ready first. There is a bathing room in your chambers, and you'll find that your clothing has been washed since last night."

The color drained from my face. I wasn't sure how I'd gotten *out* of that clothing to begin with.

Albert cleared his throat. "I can send Iris up to help you dress. Though she confessed to having a difficult time helping you last night." He chuckled as if I weren't standing in an unfamiliar place, wearing unfamiliar clothing, with the memory of a goldfish. "You insisted on doing it yourself."

"Sounds like me," I muttered, briefly looking away. "Pardon me," I began, meeting his gaze once more. "Who is Iris?"

"The maid I sent for you after we came back to the palace."

I blinked again, slowly trying to piece together each word that left his pretty mouth. "The palace," I repeated. Not a question. Not a statement, either.

Albert gestured around as if everything should have been extremely clear to me. "Well, I wasn't going to let you and your friend sleep in that Inn with how intoxicated you were. It would have been in bad taste. Do you know how dangerous it is for two young women to be in that state alone in an Inn like that?"

Fury came quickly. I didn't know if it appeared because of my embarrassment or because it seemed like he was judging me for having a good time. Either way, I was angry. "We had each other." My words came out clipped and irritated.

"Yes, well–" he chewed on his words, thinking them over carefully. Somehow, the rest of the sentence never came.

"Albert," I said. "Why am I in the palace? Also, where is Nessanine?"

He nodded, taking a step back as he cleared his throat and gestured down the hall. "Your friend is one room over–well taken care of by the palace staff. Same as you, when you arrived." He winced. "As for the palace, it is because I live here."

"You live here?"

"Yes, I live here."

"Why?" I asked.

"It is my home."

Surely, I had gone crazy. Maybe the alcohol hadn't worn off yet, or maybe I was dreaming and would soon awake in The Nuxberry Inn.

"Albert," I began again, but he held up a hand to stop me.

"I'd like you to stop calling me that."

"Fine." I tapped the side of the door, leaning casually as I pinned him with my stare. "What shall I call you then?"

"Tobias is fine. We can forget the titles or the full name. It's rather exhausting. We are friends, are we not?"

"Tobias." His name rolled off my tongue slowly like the sunrise in Fairvein. That's when it hit me–something far stronger than a carriage rolling down a hill. This felt like being caught in a rockslide somewhere on the side of one of the Agmund mountains.

"You mean to tell me–" I couldn't finish my sentence, too stunned to speak.

"The prince thing is overrated anyway." His eyes tracked my shocked expression, calculating his next move, no doubt. "Listen, I can see you're shaken. I will send Iris to assist you while you get ready, and we can talk more over breakfast."

He slipped into his casual charm, his smile wide as slight wrinkles formed near his eyes. For a prince, he seemed relaxed–nothing like how I thought the prince would be. I'd always imagined him to have an inflated ego, which I suppose he had, but this version of the prince wasn't stiff. In the tavern, he hadn't turned up his nose at his patrons, and they hadn't made his arrival a spectacle. It was as if he'd frequented the city in which he lived.

Yes, Prince Tobias Cranefield was far less like the image of a prince I'd imagined in my adulthood. His demeanor aligned far more closely with how I'd imagined him as a child. A child with a silly crush that somehow managed to keep its roots.

If I'd been right about anything–it was that the prince was jarringly handsome.

"Breakfast," I repeated, cursing myself for my sudden lack of vocabulary. "Breakfast in the palace?"

"Surely," he replied.

Tobias–not Albert–nodded once before spinning on his heel and sauntering down the hallway.

I slammed the door closed a bit too hard and found myself leaning against the thing gasping for breath.

Somehow, through the decisions we made last night, I found myself in the palace with a prince who had seen all of my drunkenness. He didn't seem like the type to take advantage of a woman–but it still had me questioning the things I may have said to him–the way I–

"Oh my," I spoke, covering my eyes with my hands as if it might do anything to fix the situation.

It only served to blind me temporarily.

I should have been happy–really. I'd spent my entire adult life trying to get close to the palace. This could turn into a great opportunity. Tobias didn't seem disgusted by my sheer lack of decency last night, and instead, he invited me to breakfast. I'd awoken in a very expensive king-sized bed surrounded by luxury, which sure beat the accommodations at the Inn.

In fact, I should have been happy that being within the palace walls got me one step closer to uncovering the truth about my father's betrayal.

I *should* have focused on using the opportunity, but my mind seemed to only want to drag up all of the inappropriate comments I made to Tobias before I'd blacked out from too much drink.

I looked down once more, noting the long, silken, emerald pants I was wearing.

It was the only explanation for my inability to focus on the puzzle that was my father's past.

I wasn't wearing my own trousers and desperately needed a bath, so I could put them back on.

Looking to the restroom attached to my overly extravagant room, I decided I would start there, find Ness, discover a way to avoid breakfast with the prince and return to the Inn– to my normal life.

After all, I had an archery competition set to start in the late afternoon, and that needed to remain my focus.

Six

"Ness!" my harsh whisper cut through the hallway as I knocked on the door, hoping Nessanine would remember more than I had.

My headache had worn off after Iris brought me a tonic and some extra water. I thanked her and told her she could take her leave. It was weird enough that I'd awoken in the palace. There was only so much luxury I could endure.

I quickly bathed, combed, and braided my hair, and donned the newly cleaned outfit I had worn the previous night.

I knocked again. "Ness, are you in there?"

"She's gone, Miss."

I spun, coming face to face with Iris again as she stood in the hallway, her brown hair pinned back neatly and her eyes warm.

"I'm so sorry," I said. "I was told she'd be there. I was just–"

Iris held up a pale hand to stop me. "Not a problem. She requested to leave earlier. Said you could join her back at the Inn when you were done with your bath. I let her know you would be attending breakfast."

I nodded, my eyes glancing toward the elaborate tapestry hanging from the wall. The sea foam color matched that of my comforter. As did the golden embroidery. The palace was clearly etched into the fabric–a mix of thread detailing each corridor.

I couldn't help but wonder what was hidden behind the palace walls—what secrets could be unearthed to point me in the right direction.

Iris cleared her throat.

I looked at her as she awaited a response, realizing I hadn't heard what she said.

"So sorry. I must have lost myself to thought. Could you repeat that?"

"Would you like escorted to breakfast?" she asked.

Looking at the tapestry once more, I realized there would be no way I'd be able to navigate the halls of the palace. For one, I'd never been in it. And even though my father's descriptions of the place had been elaborate, time had worn the memory of those stories into a moth-eaten cloth—filled with holes I couldn't repair.

I curtsied, not knowing how to conduct myself in a place so proper. "Yes," I finally replied. "Of course."

❧ ❧

"I'll leave you here. The door to the personal dining room is just through those doors at the end of the hall." Iris pointed to the double doors looming in the distance before scurrying away to attend to her duties.

My stomach twisted and pulled uncomfortably. I wasn't sure how to handle myself. If the prince had taken me riding through the forest—had asked me to shoot arrows at a target—I would have had a better idea of how to behave. In this instance, I was completely lost.

It unsettled me.

Walking toward the doors, I noticed a sliver of warm light leaking through the crack, joined by voices.

"You have duties, Tobias. Duties that cannot be avoided. You've spent this long wandering around the continent enjoying yourself, and you've still come back with little to show for it. If you won't find a wife on your own, I'll be forced to do it for you."

I halted at the authority in the woman's tone–the way she scolded him. Peeking around the corner, I saw the source–the queen, herself.

"You wouldn't force me to marry out of duty, Mother." Tobias sat casually in the chair next to her, analyzing a glass filled with what I assumed to be water. He wore the same outfit he'd been in when I saw him earlier.

"I wouldn't have a choice. I think we should host a dinner. How about that one governor's daughter? Calliope, is it?"

"No."

The queen's brows knit together as she sat straighter in her chair. "No?" she questioned. "Boy, you better have a good reason for telling me such a thing."

His eyes widened as he set the glass back down on the table with a soft clink. "I cannot meet other women from the kingdom. I'm already otherwise engaged."

Not even the servants could hide their gasp at the revelation.

I quickly covered my mouth with my hand, hoping they hadn't heard me. While I wasn't accustomed to court politics or appropriate behavior, I was fairly certain that eavesdropping would be looked down upon.

"Well, I mean–" He was fumbling. Even I knew it. The casual and collected prince could hardly piece together a sentence. "The girl–"

"The one you snuck into the guest room last night?"

Tobias cleared his throat, clearly uncomfortable as I waited for him to deny the claim.

For the love of Fairvein and all her people, I'd just met the man.

"Well, Mother. Yes."

This time, I wasn't so quiet. As I leaned forward, the door creaked, causing Tobias to glance up. When our eyes met, I saw shock first and then something else I couldn't quite put my finger on.

His chair screeched against the floors as he muttered his apologies to the queen and quickly made his way to the hallway with me, where he closed the door.

"Engaged!" I said, aghast. It was so ridiculous that I laughed a hollow and bitter sound. "You and me?"

"Please lower your voice. You couldn't possibly understand."

Anger started welling in my chest. This man—this arrogant boy believed that because he held a title and the blessing of good looks, he could manipulate me into an engagement mere days after we'd met. Did he even know my name? Was he really serious?

I folded my arms across my chest, hoping that my distaste for his behavior would somehow make him appear uglier. No luck.

"Please," I scoffed. "Explain, then."

Tobias nodded, glancing down the hall at an approaching staff member before grabbing my arm. I had the urge to pull away but refrained when his eyes met mine.

"Fine," he said. "Just not here."

We turned down a separate hall where he parted one of the tapestries lining the wall—a different one than I'd seen earlier—to reveal a small alcove.

When he dragged me inside and let the fabric drape over the hole, I nearly cursed. I was *positive* this behavior was far worse than my eavesdropping. And what if we were caught in an alcove? The man had just told his mother we were engaged!

"This is less than ideal," I ground out.

Small trickles of light leaked in from around the tapestry, painting a line across his face. For the most part, we were covered in darkness, standing far too close for my liking.

"I panicked," he admitted. "I don't want to be matched with a stranger, and I have it on good authority that my mother doesn't want to see that happen, either."

"She sure seemed like she wanted to see that happen." I was whisper-yelling. "And on what authority?"

"She's my mother. I've known her my whole life."

I rolled my eyes, huffing as I crossed my arms. The space was so crowded my forearms brushed against his chest. I simply ignored it—too irritated to think about his nearness now.

"Because knowing someone your whole life makes you the expert." Bitterness and sarcasm dripped from my tone—spilling my secrets right there in the alcove. I'd known my father my entire life, too, and he had betrayed the crown—gotten himself killed. Knowing someone didn't mean you truly *knew* them at all.

"Listen," he started. "I need you to play along with the engagement. At least for the time you're here."

"Absolutely not." I lifted my chin. "I am here for an archery competition. I'm here to compete, and that is all. I will not be paraded around like some prized pig in front of your family to help you avoid your responsibilities."

He gave me a pointed look, the corners of his mouth tugging downward. It was the first time I'd seen him frown instead of smile, and his displeasure caused me more satisfaction than I cared to admit.

"You're not just here for a competition," he began. "You'd like to be part of the guard."

I sucked in a sharp breath, my heart picking up in pace. "How do you know that?"

"You told me last night. Among other things." Tobias stepped closer, causing a woodsy scent to fill my lungs. It was something like applewood and tobacco with a touch of sweetness. "Your father betrayed the crown, Luna. If you're going to be part of the guard, you're going to need my help. For starters, you need me to keep that secret."

Panic seized my lungs, making it harder to breathe in the limited space we had. It was my deepest secret, and now it had been placed in the hands of the last person who should know it.

"You slimy little snake!" I accused, leaning toward him with rage in my heart. "You are exactly the type to take advantage of a woman."

"I didn't touch you, nor would I have even thought of it." We were so close now—so cloaked in darkness, I started wondering what that may be like until I realized that *I* had thought of it. He'd all but admitted he found me repulsive. My anger was far too strong now, and I got the sudden urge to punch the prince square in the face.

"You offered up information to *me*," he continued. "Which is exactly why I brought you to the palace. You shouldn't be wandering around drunk like that."

I scoffed, barely able to contain my irritation. "Oh, because you would know."

Something cut through his harsh expression—the easy smile returning to his face and disarming me. It was the same arrogant smirk he'd given me when we first met. "I am the prince. I know a lot about the dangers of the city. You're lucky I found you when I did."

My lip peeled back, my fingers itching to touch my bowstring. If I'd have had the weapon, I would have used it—driven an arrow straight through his heart. "Lucky you found me so you could blackmail me into this ridiculous arrangement."

"Is that what you believe I'm doing?"

Exasperated, I lifted my hands, gesturing to the air around me and hoping it would cool down the small alcove. Or maybe it would heat it up–cause the prince to pass out right here so I could escape.

"If you believe you are not blackmailing me, then I worry for your education. You are forcing me to pretend to be *engaged*. All because you found out about my father's betrayal and can hold it against me. You've used the information to threaten the one and only thing I've wanted my entire life–to be a part of the guard."

For what it was worth, Tobias had the decency to look uncomfortable–as if this was new territory for him. I got the feeling that blackmail wasn't a normal activity for him–prince or not.

"You are right." His shoulders deflated as he leaned away–as far as he could lean given the space. "I will make up for it–I swear. I just need you to do me this favor, and I promise. The position on the guard will be yours, Luna."

Luna. Something about the way he said my name made my cheeks flush. He was really quite good–even if he *was* a snake.

As far as I saw it, I had no choice. He was promising me the very thing I wanted–to get the position I'd always dreamed of. And to be fair, a short engagement was a small price to pay for such a gift. Besides, Tobias now knew the truth, and while that detail frightened me, I knew that *he* was still *pretending* to be engaged to a commoner. He'd hold the secret while it benefited him–that I knew.

There was also something freeing about it. Maybe he could help me. I might be able to be honest about my search–and the prince would certainly know where to look. He may even know what had happened. Maybe he even knew my father.

"Fine," I conceded. "I will pretend to be engaged to you for the two weeks I am in Draymore. But I expect to be hired on the guard promptly after we call off our engagement."

His smile widened, and my traitorous heart beat on the side of *too quickly*.

"You've got yourself a–"

Footsteps sounded in the hallway just beyond the tapestry, causing me to turn, but Tobias quickly pulled me close, clasping a warm hand over my mouth and holding my back to his chest.

My mind was spinning–drunk on the scent of him, but fearful of being caught. If we were really to fake an engagement, this would be the worst position to be found in. While we were merely participating in blackmail, lies, and manipulation, the staff would assume the worst–spread the lies through the kingdom.

I felt his breath hot on my neck when he leaned down, my body suddenly buzzing with the nearness of him as the footsteps retreated.

"You've got yourself a deal," he whispered before uncovering my mouth.

I gave him a harsh look–one that longed to bury whatever strange feelings his touch brought upon me. "I'm skipping breakfast," I declared before promptly leaving the alcove and finding my way to the nearest staff member who could escort me out.

SEVEN

When I arrived at the Inn, after a very long walk, I stomped my way up the creaking wooden steps and through the dimly lit hallway until I found Nessanine's door.

After knocking once, the door swung open to reveal Ness–put together as always–with a stunned look on her face. Eyes wide and mouth hanging open, she froze for a moment before dragging me into her room and slamming the door.

"The prince!" she practically shrieked. "The man you met on the ferry was the prince!" She began pacing the room, wooden floors groaning with every step of her well-shined boots. "You mean to tell me that last night we got drunk, and I said that the prince, Tobias Cranefield, smelled like a good romp."

I hadn't moved from my position near the door, still standing still as Nessanine threw herself on the bed. Her cheeks were pink, and her flawless appearance began to show a crack of embarrassment.

I cleared my throat, my stomach twisting at the thought of what I'd share next.

"That's not the worst part," I muttered.

Nessanine shot up from her position on the bed, causing the metal to squeal. I winced, regretting the fact that I was thankful for sleeping in a nicer bed at the palace before the competition.

"How is that not the worst part, Luna?"

I stepped forward, finding my seat next to her on the bed. "Well," I began, just as unsure of how to broach the subject as I was unsure of the rules regarding conduct in the palace. "We are engaged."

Nessanine grabbed my hand. "Forgive me," she said, somewhat breathless. "I may vomit."

I sprang from the bed, running to grab the waste bin from the corner. The trash goblins would certainly be disgruntled when they found a bag of vomit tonight, but it was far better than allowing Ness to throw up on the scratchy, cream-colored sheets.

"Here." I handed her the bin which she took gladly.

"It's not real," I declared. "His mother had been pressuring him to marry. He didn't enjoy the pressure. He told her a lie I overheard, and I agreed to go along with it after he blackmailed me."

Her brows pulled into a quizzical expression. "The prince black-mailed you?"

"Ness." My voice was barely a whisper, the reality of my situation crashing into me all at once. My deepest secret had found the light, and there was nothing I could do to control where it went next. In a way, I was placing all of my trust in the Prince of Edessa. A scary thought, to be sure.

"He knows about my father."

I closed my eyes, hoping to block out whatever horrified expression had appeared on her face after the news. Nessanine knew the seri-ousness of the situation. She'd been my friend for as long as I could remember. Closer than anyone save for Woodrow.

As the thought crossed my mind, I felt a longing in my chest. I longed for Woodrow's small farmhouse and the fields in Fairvein. I wanted to escape–move somewhere safer than the continent. The continent had been an escape. Edessa was a place I could build a name for myself–craft something new–but Fairvein was the place where I could be truly known. Even if it was only a few who knew—it still mattered. I didn't know if the continent could ever provide that for me—not when it felt like the place that took my father.

I opened my eyes, noting that Nessanine was frowning—concerned.

"What are you going to do?"

I shrugged, trying to hide my dissatisfaction. It didn't matter, anyway. I had no choice.

"Well," I said. "I'm going to spend the next two weeks pretending to be engaged to the prince of Edessa. I'm going to win the archery competition, and I will find myself working for the royal guard at the end of it all." I tried to muster a smile. "Easy."

It was *not* easy.

"*That* is what he decided to hang over your head? A position on the guard."

"He holds a position where that wouldn't be so difficult for him. I suppose it's a small price to pay." I found my way back to the spot next to her on the bed, now sure that she wouldn't lose her breakfast all over me. The sunlight streamed through the window, highlighting the dust floating around the Inn.

"A small price to pay, my ass! Will you have to kiss him?"

My face twisted at the question. It wasn't something we had discussed. Though I was furious with Tobias, I couldn't imagine that kissing him would be all that unpleasant. "He didn't say."

Nessanine sighed, placing the waste bin on the floor. "At least he's charming."

I chuckled. Leaning my head on her shoulder and staring at the bare wall of her room. A smile crossed my lips, and I was thankful that this time it wasn't forced. I'd be forcing many smiles in the coming weeks. It was an activity I loathed entirely.

"Yes," I finally said. "At least there's that."

After leaving Nessanine, I found my way back to my room. The bedding sat untouched, and my belongings remained safe in the corner.

I knelt by one of my bags, pulling a stopwatch from one of the pockets. The smooth gold of the clock felt cold against my fingers, but the subtle tick brought me a sense of comfort. It had been my father's–given to me by my mother after he passed.

"Three more hours," I whispered to myself.

When a knock sounded at the door, I turned, watching as a piece of paper slipped through the bottom crack and halted just on my side.

I picked it up, noting the golden wax seal and the foiled accents around the envelope.

Upon opening the letter, my suspicions were confirmed.

It was from the palace.

Dearest Luna,

I have written to inform you that my mother expects an official announcement at the opening ceremony tonight. I do apologize for the inconvenience. I know you longed to focus on the archery tournament and not our–entanglement.

My mother was disappointed that you were unable to attend breakfast. I promised you would be in attendance tomorrow morning. The queen hosts a tea once a week, and she's looking forward to your attendance tomorrow. I will send you something to wear this evening. Please be advised that my mother is a fan of large hats.

I will speak to you prior to the opening ceremony. We must go over expectations.

Yours,

Tobias

I stared at the letter. Dread filling my lungs with every breath I took. I didn't know if it was the situation or the state of the Inn.

Either way, it was uncomfortable.

And either way, I'd found myself in a strange predicament.

Tomorrow morning, I'd be dining with the queen.

As the prince's fiancée.

EIGHT

While Fairvein had remained my home base through my adulthood, I always found its culture to be somewhat intrusive. That is to say that one's business belonged to the entire town, and though everyone was well-meaning, it was still a bit unsettling.

It seemed that the sentiment was not confined to the island of Fairvein.

As I carefully finished braiding my hair, standing in the grass just behind the shooting line, I found myself the subject of whispers and stares. Some were harmless enough, but others were downright nasty. No doubt from women who had dreams of falling in love with Prince Cranefield.

I had to stop myself from telling them it wouldn't be worth it.

With my hair properly braided, I adjusted my leather armguard, tightening the strap over my gray sleeve. I wore a simple shirt instead of a sweater despite the bite in the air. Draymore's climate wasn't nearly as mild as Fairvein or the cities on the southern end of the continent. Located north near the Agmund mountains, Draymore was decorated with evergreen trees and a constant wind that brought the mountain snow chill with it. I didn't mind—in fact, I found it quite pleasant.

Besides, with all the stares and whispers I was receiving, my embarrassment was enough to keep me warm. My cheeks were tinted pink for certain.

When a spot cleared, I grabbed my bow off one of the hooks embedded into the wooden stand and stepped up to the line.

Different targets were spaced out equally, with wooden signs painted to detail the distance at which we were shooting. I don't know why I did it—maybe it was because I was frustrated with the attention. Attention due to my affiliation with the prince—despite the announcement being scheduled for later in the day—frustrated me. I wanted the guests and other competitors to pay attention to my skill—my talent.

I picked out the sixty-yard target—much too far for a first shot while warming up. Nocking my arrow, I kept my eyes pinned to the center, the world and noise of the crowds in the stands and the other competitors all but disappearing. When I drew back, I felt the pull of my bowstring—the tension that had been the cause of sore muscles all growing up. I no longer felt that muscle's soreness, but I could feel the memory of it—as if every aspect of the sport had been etched into the fibers of my being.

Breathing deeply, I lined up the shot, slowly pulling my elbow back until I felt the gentle release of the arrow—sent flying across the grass and plummeting directly in the center of the sixty-yard target.

Satisfied, I took a moment to look around.

Instead of impressed gasps and gaping mouths, I was met with rolling eyes and irritated stares.

My stomach twisted, and I frowned.

Without bothering to retrieve my arrow, I gripped my bow tighter, turning around to see Tobias standing next to his mother and father in their very extravagant spot in the stands. When our eyes met, I glared at him before stocking off to go to my room within the walls of the stadium.

Pacing my room in the stadium seemed to help–if only a little.

I needed a moment to get my head on straight–figure out if the entire fake engagement was even worth discovering my father's secrets. As for my position on the guard, I was sure everyone in all of Edessa would be firstly, confused, and secondly, irritated because they would believe I got the position through association with the prince.

They weren't wrong.

A knock sounded at the door, and I ceased attempting to form a rut through the center of the room.

Figuring it was Nessanine, I turned around to count the arrows I had left after leaving mine for dead.

"Come in," I hollered toward the door, listening as it creaked open and promptly shut.

"I'm actually glad you're here. I don't think I can go through with it, Ness. The stares–the assumptions." I closed my eyes, dropping my quiver and praying to anyone who would listen. "I used to be known for my talent, not my association with some sneaky, lying prince. I simply cannot."

"Then don't," his deep voice took me by surprise, and I spun, finding Prince Cranefield standing by the closed door, his jacket and trousers looking rather expensive for an archery tournament. My eyes met the arrow in his hand–the one I'd left behind.

When he held it out to me, I snatched it up, taking a step back to place more distance between us.

"You can't mean that," I finally said, and he stepped forward.

"I mean it."

It was then that I noticed how disheveled he looked–as if he'd been contemplating his life decisions and realizing he'd made a horrible mistake.

I guessed I was the mistake.

Tobias cleared his throat. "I'm sorry I put you in this position, Luna." His gentle tone was a balm to my anger and swirling nerves. "I shouldn't have forced you into an engagement, and you're right. The whispers are out of control, and my mother has yet to announce anything."

My heart fluttered, my palms quickly growing sweaty. "You don't think–" Worry kept me in its claws as I lowered my voice. "You don't think someone saw us?" I asked. "In the alcove?"

He chuckled, running a hand over his cropped hair. "I don't believe so. And even if they had, we weren't doing anything but arguing."

My mind drifted to how solid his chest felt against my back–how hot his breath had been on my neck.

I shook off the feeling. "Yes, of course." Returning my arrow to the quiver, I longed for something to do to distract from my complicated feelings.

I turned, realizing he seemed to have more to say.

"Well," I began. "Why the change of heart?"

Tobias took another step forward, a certain longing on his face. "I want to explain. I am not normally like this–the blackmailing and such. I partook in my fair share of mischief as a child, but I'm not a monster."

A breathy laugh left my lips. "I don't believe you to be a monster, Tobias."

"Good!" His voice was on the side of too loud. He quickly cleared his throat and recovered. "Good, yes. Anyway, I've come to apologize and allow you the chance to back out of our arrangement."

Ice coated my veins. The man knew my deepest secret–he held my future in his hands whether we pretended to be engaged or not. "And what of your knowledge of my father?" I asked.

His brows pushed together, concern shining in his brown eyes. "Luna," he said. "You really believe I would share such information? That I would prevent you from joining the guard–if that is what you really want?"

"I–" I found myself at a loss for words. Still, my whole life had been filled with uncertainty. The only constant from the time I was thirteen was my bow–my arrows. "I don't know," I finally admitted.

Tobias took another step forward, the concern deepening the lines on his face. He was rather close now, but I didn't back away from him.

"I would *never* let the conduct of your parents determine your worth. It is not as if I hadn't heard of you before our meeting in Fairvein. You're a talented archer, Luna. The guard would be lucky to have you."

Something in my chest warmed, and I felt my eyes becoming damp at the words that left his lips. It was ridiculous, really, so I blinked it away.

Tobias seemed to notice the shift as the corners of his mouth drew upward into his famous smirk–the one I had now become so familiar with. This one reminded me of the man I met in Birdie's shop. Confident–undoubtedly likable.

"I, for one, would feel extremely safe with my life held in your hands."

It was meant to be a placating joke, but my heart skipped all the same.

"Thank you, Tobias." My voice came out a mere whisper.

He stared at me for a moment–so close I found it hard to breathe. "Answer this for me first," he began. "Why did your father betray the crown? I remember him, you know. He didn't seem like the type."

Looking away, I quickly tried to gather my thoughts–how much I wanted to confess to the prince. I settled on the truth. "I'm not entirely sure," I admitted. "My hope was that our engagement would afford me an opportunity to figure it out."

"Ah," he said, and I could hear the smile in his voice. "I'm starting to believe I was the one ensnared by you, Miss Ellsworth."

My eyes snapped to his, noting the humor there. "I did not blackmail you. if that's what you're thinking, Prince Cranefield."

"Tobias is fine," he said. "And you certainly did not blackmail me, but you were prepared to use my fortune and status to your advantage."

I should have been angry, but the amusement radiating from me halted that emotion in its tracks. "You're welcome to marry any of the women who have been giving me dirty looks in the stadium instead." My own smile cut across my face. "I'm sure they would be far nobler than I."

I suddenly became aware of how closely we stood, his scent wrapping around me and making me dizzy. "I highly doubt that."

A moment of silence passed between us—charged like a summer storm streaking lightning across the sky.

Without moving, I asked the question that had been on the tip of my tongue. "What of your mother?"

Tobias chuckled, a sound that was quickly burrowing beneath my skin. "I will deal with her. And I want to offer my help in finding out any information I can about your father—free of charge."

I stared at him, my mind wanting to doubt him, but my heart trusting all the same. I knew that Fairvein had been filled with good people, and something about Tobias Cranefield made me believe that the continent could provide the same.

And maybe that was the secret of not only the island, but of humanity. Kindness begot kindness.

"I don't mind," I finally said. "Pretending to be engaged. I do not mind if it would help your situation."

Tobias smiled wider than–an expression that seemed to light up the room.

"Are you proposing to me, Luna Ellsworth?"

I chuckled, unable to keep my own smile from widening in response. "Yes," I finally said, looking up to meet his gaze. "But only for a short while."

"Then it's settled."

The door opened, startling us both, and I once again realized how close we were standing to one another.

The woman at the door seemed a bit shocked to find us there, her eyes quickly gluing themselves to the prince.

"Excuse me," she said, her pale skin flushed as if she'd been running–her breath short. "The opening ceremony begins in just a few minutes."

Though I was certain she was speaking to me, her eyes never went back to me. I couldn't blame her.

"Yes, of course." I found myself somewhat flustered–realizing what our position looked like–and how it would look following the announcement.

Tobias, for what it was worth, didn't seem nervous at all. "I will leave you to it," he said, his casual charm returning in full force. "Good luck out there."

He placed a gentle kiss on my temple before taking his leave, shocking both the woman at the door and my heart.

When the room was finally empty of all other guests, I grabbed my bow, wondering why the spot where his lips had met my skin still burned hot.

Nine

The opening ceremony for the archery competition consisted of showcasing our skill, introducing the competitors, and announcing the prize money.

I'd done well—pleased with my performance despite the reception of my score. As planned, our engagement was announced, making the stares and whispering far worse. Though, by the time it occurred, it bothered me far less. I didn't believe Tobias to be a monster or a snake, as I had called him before.

To be perfectly honest, he was kind.

It was that thought that followed me in the carriage from The Nuxberry Inn and all the way to the palace.

An emerald gown had been sent to my room, lush and far more expensive than anything I typically wore. The sleeves were sheer and off the shoulder—the bodice sloping into a gentle sweetheart neckline that accentuated my collarbones. As for the skirt, delicate vines and flowers decorated the fabric beneath another sheer layer of green—much like the sleeves.

As promised, I also found a matching hat—so large I worried it would spill out of the carriage and assault anyone and everyone mulling in the streets.

The dress, though not trousers, was beautiful.

The hat—

When the carriage rolled to a stop, the footman, a human, opened the door and offered me his hand. I took it, knowing that the skirt would be an adjustment, as I dismounted the few steps to the ground.

Guards stood at the door, their faces covered by the sheer masks they wore–swords and bows strapped to their backs and ready should something go amiss.

My chest tugged at the site–remembering my father's uniform–dirty upon his return to the island when he wasn't working.

Swallowing my emotions, my eyes caught a familiar face on the steps, ready to retrieve me. Iris stood with her hands clasped and a smile plastered to her face as the footman delicately draped my cloak over my shoulders.

When Iris curtsied, my eyes widened, surprised at the formal greeting.

"That's unnecessary," I said as she rose.

"Oh, but it isn't. You are engaged to the prince, Lady Ellsworth. It is of the utmost importance."

I followed as she gestured for us to go inside the palace, leaning down to whisper. "But if we are ever in private," I said. "Please treat me normally. It is odd–beyond odd–to be treated so formally."

Iris chuckled, her pale hand coming up to cover her mouth. "You are perfect for Prince Cranefield, I'm afraid. One in the same."

The words struck me, calling up more feelings I'd had in his presence the last we spoke–feelings I'd promised myself I wouldn't have.

Unfortunately, it was too late.

I hardly remembered the winding hallways and numerous decorations as we floated through the castle. It was all I could do to keep up.

"Queen Cranefield hosts her weekly tea in the greenhouse. It is one of her favorite times each week. She quite enjoys the view of the evergreens and the Agmund Mountains from the third floor."

"Excuse me," I interrupted. "The greenhouse is on the third floor?"

Iris chuckled again, keeping her eyes forward. "No, no. The greenhouse, itself, has five floors in total."

"Right," I whispered.

We arrived at a large wooden door, carvings of vines and various plants etched into the surface. My nerves began taking over my limbs—causing me to sweat in odd places. It worried me because I didn't want to, one, be embarrassed, and two, ruin the dress I'd been sent.

"I'll admit, my mother's affinity for large hats is a strange one at best."

I turned, watching Tobias kindly dismiss Iris and move to stand next to me. His cream-colored shirt was open to reveal the slightest hint of his chest, rings decorating his fingers, and his most essential accessory on full display—his smile.

"I'll admit that I agree with you, Prince Cranefield."

"I insist that you call me Tobias in instances like this. It would be strange for you to call me anything else." He leaned in, bumping my shoulder with his and causing a spark of heat to scale through my veins and right to my heart. "Well, *my darling* may be the exception to that rule."

I laughed too loudly on account of my nervousness. Even so, his lighthearted banter helped ease the tension. "Are you to attend tea with us?"

He winked, his hand finding mine at my side. "Oh, certainly. I attend almost every week. I quite enjoy the gossip. My father comes when he can, too. Unfortunately, he's too in love with my mother to ask her to eradicate the strange dress code."

He flicked the bill of my hat, staring down at me with such joy in his gaze I couldn't help but feel it, too.

"Shall we?" he asked, and I found myself nodding in agreement.

We walked up flights of stairs before finding ourselves on the third floor where Queen Cranefield's tea had been set up. A long table filled with pastries and small sandwiches stretched through the center of the room, ending just before a carved fountain releasing a steady trickle of water.

All eyes found us when we arrived, flicking between myself and Tobias. There must have been at least ten women in the room, a mix of elves, humans, witches, and more.

My nerves spiked again, and I was suddenly thankful for the way Tobias had held my hand the entire way through the greenhouse. He hadn't let go once. It was that warm grasp that steadied me when his mother stood from the end of the table and turned to face us, her brown skin glowing in the pink light from the day's sun. Her black hair hung in braids to her waist, and a bright orange hat matching her dress sat atop her head.

It wasn't until she smiled that I felt some of my nerves settle.

"My son's best-kept secret!" she said by way of introduction. "You're stunning, Lady Ellsworth. We are so happy to have you join us for tea this morning." She walked from her spot to wrap me in a warm hug. Tobias hadn't let go of my hand for the whole interaction.

When she pulled back, I saw true joy in her eyes and a stab of guilt struck me. We were *lying* to the queen.

"Please, please," she began. "Find a seat. We have many of my friends from over the years, but Calliope may be close to your age." She pointed to the pale woman seated nearest the fountain, two empty chairs across from her. "She is the daughter of one of our governors here in Edessa."

The queen turned, leaning toward Tobias and lowering her voice. "I'm terribly sorry," she said. "I planned her arrival before I knew."

"It's no problem, Mother." Tobias hugged her, holding my hand tightly as we walked to the end of the table to find our seats.

"Your former betrothed?" I commented, cocking an eyebrow in his direction.

"I'm sure she's lovely," he whispered. "But I fear I do not know her."

I lowered my voice in return, leaning in to continue our private conversation as we walked the length of the table. I was certain we looked in love by the way we spoke intimately. It was a good show, at the very least.

"You do not know me, *my darling*."

He lifted my hand, placing a gentle kiss there before speaking. "I know enough, Miss Luna Ellsworth."

My cheeks heated, leaving me speechless as we sat to dine with the rest of the party. Quickly pouring our tea and laughing along with the guests. The queen told stories of her friends and her son, radiating such love for her kingdom and family I found myself pulled in–realizing a piece of my soul that had been missing since the loss of my father, and later, my mother.

I had been missing family–and somewhere between scones and pastries, tea and coffee, I found myself feeling the slightest longing for what Prince Tobias Cranefield had–a home.

Ten

"My mother loved you." Tobias leaned against the wooden table at the center of the library, the gentle glow of candlelight flickering over his skin.

I'd left breakfast feeling a mix of sheer joy and deep sorrow, quickly changing into my new trousers from Birdies's shop and a simple shirt before the competition. During the course, I'd performed well, finding a letter from Tobias waiting for me in my room at the stadium.

He'd invited me to the palace to search the library for records–hoping to help me understand my Father's temperament and time on the guard.

It was now late, the sun long since disappearing from the sky during the shortening autumn days. It was darker in the library; lanterns and candlelight used to illuminate the darkness.

While I appreciated his comment, something about it brought that pain back. "The lights in the libraries," I said, avoiding the subject as best I could. "You've used fire."

Disappointment crossed his features–just briefly. My avoidance of the topic of his family seemed to be the wrong move.

"They're bewitched. One of the witches located on your island, actually. The fire won't harm the books. My father liked the ambiance of it."

I nodded, realizing that his voice sounded sadder than it had moments ago. I desperately longed to fix it. "I see why the country has such good opinions of your family," I said. "After meeting your mother, that is."

That seemed to cure the shift in his demeanor.

"Well, not all," he admitted, turning to run his fingers along the spines of some of the books. "You remember what happened to my mother in Fairvein the spring before last?"

I nodded, recalling the celebration I'd heard about at the castle where the queen had announced the winners of her yearly travel brochure. She'd chosen Fairvein that year, causing quite the uptick in excitement from the town—especially when I heard she had arrived at the Royal's summer house on the island.

"I wasn't in Fairvein at the time, but I heard of it. Isla played a rather important role, if I recall."

I ran my fingers along the wood of the table, unsure of what we were actually doing in the library. So far, we'd only marched to the center and talked.

"You're friends with her?" he asked, turning to face me. "Isla, that is."

I chuckled, the breathy sound caught by the numerous pages and spines on the shelves. "We are acquainted," I admitted. "I have no complaints about her, but I'm not nearly as close with her as I am with Nessanine."

"Ah." Tobias stood for a second, the ghost of a smirk painting his full lips. "Well, we should get started. We will need to go into the records section—restricted—so unfortunately, you'll be stuck with me for the duration of our time here."

I offered a small smile. "I can think of a worse fate."

It didn't take long for Tobias to locate the guard's record kept by the palace staff. Apparently, they found it worth their time to keep records of those who worked for them. Though most records were sparse, if any infraction occurred, it would be in the book for later reference.

Unfortunately, my father had no documentation of misconduct before his betrayal of the crown—even so, I found myself asking what he had actually done—a mystery I had long held on to.

"What does it say?" I sat beside him, looking over his shoulder at the book on the wooden table of the restricted section. The hour had grown quite late, but I didn't mind. The thrill of learning something about my past energized me.

Tobias's brows furrowed. "Strange," he murmured, pointing to the place he was reading. I quickly followed along, soaking up the words that had been carved into the page.

When I was done, I looked up to find Tobias just as confused. "He'd attempted to poison the queen?" I asked, recalling our previous conversation about what had happened at the summer palace. "Just like that guard."

"That's why it's so strange." Tobias hesitated before resting his hand gently over mine, his thumb stroking the back of my hand. "Luna," he said, his tone soft but serious. "I don't want to offend you, but did your father ever speak of organized meetings? Was there ever a hint at meeting with rebels or something of the like?"

My heart beat faster as I tried to piece together my memories, though I couldn't recall anything of the sort. "Not that I'm aware of," I admitted, my shoulders deflating in disappointment.

"It's just odd that the attempts would be so similar—both an attack on my mother, as well."

I nodded, silence passing between us as I realized he hadn't stopped caressing my hand. A flush crept up my neck as I pulled away, clearing my throat. "Well, that was–" I couldn't stop the way my chest seemed to crack open, the tears threatening to spill from my eyes. It wasn't often I allowed myself to cry–to show emotion like this, but it wasn't often I truly let someone in. Tobias knew my secrets–the heartbreak became safe in light of that. "That was, unfortunately, useless." I quickly wiped my eyes and attempted to suck the tears back up. I was being ridiculous.

"It's not over yet," he said, hope woven into the words. "I'm sure we can learn something else. I *do* remember your father, you know. Not much, but enough."

My eyes whipped upward, meeting his gaze. "What do you remember about him?" My voice was nearly breathless.

Tobias chuckled, tapping a ringed finger on the surface of the book. "I hadn't talked to him much, but he always caught me playing pranks on my mother and father. The palace is filled with secret passages that I haven't gone into in years. They were quite fun."

I laughed, my emotions settling. "Did he scold you?"

"Oh, certainly. It was a common occurrence." Slight wrinkles formed at the corners of his eyes, and I felt the sudden urge to touch them–feel the years of laughter he'd experienced in the place he'd called home.

I shook the feeling away. "You should take me some time. To see them?" When I looked back at him, he didn't seem opposed to the idea. "Maybe we could participate in more mischief."

Something about the way he leaned in, the way he sat so close without a care in the world, stirred in my belly, warming me from the inside out.

"Luna," he said, his voice low in the quiet of the library. "I would like nothing more than to get up to some mischief with you."

Eleven

Not once in all of my years competing had I missed a target during one of the competitions. It was unheard of–preposterous–a complete myth.

And yet–

As I sat furiously unlacing my boots, I kept tracing over the target I had missed earlier in the morning when the day's competition had begun. Each day for the past week, since my tea with Queen Cranefield, I'd awoken to have breakfast with Nessanine, competed favorably, and spent time at the palace with Tobias following the day's activities.

Everything had been perfect despite our lack of progress regarding my father's involvement with treason. I would even say that Tobias and I had become friends–at the very least.

So, when I found my mind wandering to the way he'd brushed his thumb across my cheek in the palace's greenhouse, to the way he'd looked so intent on kissing me the night before–

I dropped my arm.

My arrow glanced off the bottom of the target and disappeared into the dirt of the stadium floor.

I could still hear the gasps sounding through the arena–feel my failure.

"Lu?"

My door creaked open, and I grunted, hoping Nessanine would take that as her warm welcome. When I finished the last of the laces on my tall boots, I yanked them off, tossing them on the floor across the room.

"Oh, yikes," Nessanine said, finding her way to sit next to me on the floor, our backs against the metal frame of the bed.

"I've been distracted," I admitted—furious at myself for letting it happen. The woman on the ferry who had no time for love of men or anything of the sort had long since disappeared, and I was beginning to think I needed to find her.

Feelings formed—unbidden—despite my knowledge that our engagement was a sham.

"Would you like to go to dinner with me? Let off some steam?" Nessanine rested her head on my shoulder. "I promise I won't give you alcohol. It didn't go so well the last time."

I huffed an amused breath. "It certainly did not go well." Massaging my temples, I tried to devise a plan—solve the puzzle that had become of my wandering heart. It wandered as much as I had on the continent for these competitions, always longing for home and never truly finding it.

My goals were all I had.

"I will need to pass on dinner. I'm meant to meet Tobias at the palace." I sighed. I'd have to speak with him—tell him I needed space—*something*.

Ness hummed, keeping her head firmly secured to my shoulder. "It may not be such a bad thing, you know. The distraction."

I pulled away, shooting daggers in her direction. "What a ridiculous thing to say."

"You're very driven, Luna. you've spent most of your life reaching for this goal. So much so that you've blocked everyone out. The only true relationships you have are with Woodrow and me. Aren't you lonely?"

It hurt–what she was saying.

After that first tea with the queen, I'd become aware of the pieces I was missing. While I didn't want to admit it, Ness had a point. I wasn't even certain I wanted to be on the guard anymore. It was merely something I was good at–a way to feel closer to someone I'd never truly known.

Postponing the discussion seemed like the right decision, though.

"I appreciate you, Ness." Grabbing her hand, I squeezed a little harder than normal. "I want you to know that."

A knowing smirk painted her lips. "Not wanting to talk about it?"

I offered a smile to match hers. "Not in the slightest."

She nodded, understanding that I needed time to process my feelings–the giant complication that had become my life.

"Breakfast tomorrow?" I asked.

"Yes, but you're buying," she joked. "Your nearness to the prince means you have plenty of coin to spare."

I laughed, the frustration slowly receding, leaving only love for my closest friend in its wake.

The palace greeted me against a backdrop of snow-capped mountains and sprawling evergreens surrounding the gates and unfurling like a blanket toward a vast country I'd spent my adult life seeing.

It was terrifying that the sentiment no longer appealed to me.

Ness was right–it was lonely traveling the continent on my own.

"You seem worried." Tobias stood at the entrance, ready for my arrival.

I'd been sent a number of dresses following the opening day of the competition. Thankfully, I'd also received no more hats.

For this particular meeting, I wasn't sure what we'd be doing–though most of our days were spent walking the grounds and appearing to be in love–talking as Tobias wrapped his hand around mine and discussed his family, his life growing up, and his hopes for the kingdom.

I'd chosen a light blue dress for the occasion. The corseted bodice clung to my figure until the skirt sprawled out delicately all the way to the floor.

Tobias wore a white jacket with gold embroidery–looking very much like a handsome prince.

I found myself nervous in his presence. The pretending had gone to my head, I supposed.

"I missed my target today," I admitted, refusing to meet his eyes. "I'm sure you witnessed it. I haven't done that in a competition since I was a kid."

He chuckled, the sound light and echoing through the entrance to the palace, traveling up the elaborate staircase ahead of us. "Your score is so high; I don't believe it will cost you your win. In case that was your worry."

My eyes snapped to his, and he must have read the disappointment on my face.

"I'm so sorry, Luna. Do you know why you missed the target?"

Wincing, I found myself staring at the ground again. "I was distracted," I mumbled, unwilling to discuss the almost kiss or the way I felt about it. Tobias had been nothing but kind to me, but this arrangement was temporary–pretend. We were friends, surely, but there were no feelings from him. I couldn't stand the embarrassment.

"I dropped my arm," I finished.

Tobias hummed, grabbing my hand in a way that had become so familiar–sending a shot of warmth up my arm. "Well," he began. "I suppose a pleasant distraction is in order."

"A walk through the palace?" I guessed. "Should we discuss cake flavors–just to sell the ruse? I shall recommend Cyris's bake shop on the island of Fairvein, and you can complain that by the time the cake found us, it would be a dry and disgusting lump of icing." I chuckled, staring at the amusement in his brown eyes. "Then we shall be like a real couple."

I regretted saying it, but Tobias hadn't shown he noticed–nor did he realize the feelings trapped just behind the words.

"We can still argue about cake if you'd like. However, our walk through the palace will be more–" he paused, trying to find the right word. "*Private.*"

Butterflies took flight in the pit of my belly–so frantic I began to wonder if they'd had a strongly caffeinated tea earlier in the day.

"Yes," I said, my voice smaller than I would have liked. "Well, lead the way."

Twelve

"I promise I'm not kidnapping you," Tobias assured as he pulled the large painting off the wall of one of the guest bedrooms we'd found ourselves in.

We'd snuck in, glancing around the hallway before entering to refrain from unpleasant gossip.

"That was actually my first assumption," I said with a smile. We'd long since settled into our normal routine, my worries fading at the warmth in his eyes, how easy it was to talk to him. The discussion about our upcoming split sat in a far corner of my mind, but it was still important all the same. I needed to be rid of my distracting feelings—cut ties with the prince in a way that would cause the least amount of scandal.

When the painting lowered, I noted the small door nestled into the palace wall—hidden in plain sight.

I shot forward, anxious to get a better look. "What is this?" I asked—too afraid to touch the door.

Tobias had a satisfied smile plastered to his face—as if he had just discovered the cure for every illness on the continent. "It's an entrance to the secret tunnels I told you about. I hope you're ready for some mischief, Luna."

Excitement buzzed in my veins as he carefully opened the door to reveal a long hallway, dark and mysterious–full of secrets to be uncovered.

"We will need to bring a light," I observed. Tobias snapped his fingers, a glowing light appearing just above his hand. My eyes widened.

Though I was an elf, I didn't hold the same magic that others held. Most of the time, the magic was mild–nothing like some of the witches that dwelled within the forests around Edessa. Even so, it wasn't abnormal for the elven people to have *some* magic.

"Don't be too impressed," Tobias said, humor laced through his tone. "This is about the only thing I can do."

I patted his firm chest before ducking into the secret passageway. "I highly doubt that," I responded. "I'm sure you're good at a great many things."

His nervous laughter sounded behind me as we made our way into the darkness–lit only by the light he had conjured.

When the door closed behind us, the echoes of our footsteps and the feeling of one another's company were the only things to remain.

In the brief silence, I found that it was as good a time as any to bring up the worries I'd had since this morning.

"We will no longer be engaged in a few days," I said, trying to gauge his feelings on the matter. "Should we stage a dramatic break-up? Bring scandal to the kingdom? I'm sure a great many women will be most pleased with our downfall."

He hummed as if thinking. "Unfortunately, I am not interested in any of those women."

Thankful for the darkness, I fought off the hope that his words gave me. "You've found a real contender then? Someone you wish to court?"

We turned down another hall, walking until we made our way to a grate leaking light into the passageway.

"The kitchens," he whispered, kneeling on the ground below. "The kitchen staff always has the best gossip."

I knelt down to join him, careful not to step on the skirt of my dress.

Peering into the large room, I noted a flurry of people plating various courses. The smell caused my stomach to growl. I hadn't had time to eat before my arrival and was now aware of my state of hunger.

"As for your question about someone to court, I believe I've found someone worth courting." Disappointment wrapped around me like vines choking out the hope of it all. "Though, I must admit I've had little experience courting women despite my rather compelling appearance." He smiled, wicked and proud. "You could possibly give me some advice."

I swallowed my pride. "Of course. Though I can't promise that I won't poke fun at your ideas and lack of experience." I thought of a simpler time–our time on the ferry, where I'd had no real knowledge of what would become of me and the stranger I met in Birdie's shop. "Friends occasionally insult one another in jest, do they not?"

He laughed, drawing the attention of one of the cooks who promptly made her way to the vent. "Tobias Cranefield, have you no decency? You are an adult, get out of the tunnels, you–"

She didn't finish the insult, instead, slapping the vent with a towel that startled us both. We shot up, laughing as we ran deeper into the tunnels, high on the thrill of getting caught.

Stopping outside of another small door, I clutched my chest, fighting to catch my breath. "You really did make a name for yourself as a child," I mused.

Tobias laughed, looking back toward the way we'd come. "Edith hasn't changed a bit," he said. "Have you eaten?"

"No, I came right to the palace as soon as I could. I couldn't keep the prince waiting."

Tobias's smile widened. "Perfect," he said, turning to open the door.

The sound of glass rolling stole our attention, a jar left abandoned in the secret passageways tucked within the palace walls.

"What's that?" I asked.

"I'm not entirely sure," he said. "We don't use these corridors. Possibly something I left as a child. I suppose mixing up potions that did not work was something I would have done."

I peered at the glass, using the light he still had hovering near us.

"It's rather clean for something so old."

"Well, you know," he began. "If nobody uses these, I suppose it's been left untouched." The door opened, dim light flooding into the darkness from a small section of the greenhouse—tinted green by the plants covering the door.

"Come on," he said. "We have to pass through this jungle first, but I have something prepared."

I took one more look at the bottle before following him. While we hadn't discussed the details of our ending engagement, I wasn't rushed to continue the conversation—too distracted by my hunger and the way the prince's behind appeared in his trousers.

THIRTEEN

We stood on the first floor of the greenhouse, just past the plants that had blocked our entrance. In the center, near a flowing waterfall draped over natural rock, sat a small blanket, a basket, and two flute glasses. Twinkling lights had been strung around the picnic area, providing light in the slowly darkening evening.

My brow furrowed, heart pounding a steady rhythm in my chest. Its beating was the only thing I could be certain of.

"What is this?" I asked, keeping my eyes on what appeared to be a picnic setting placed at the center of the greenhouse.

Lush plants climbed upward, stretching toward the memory of the late autumn sun that shone through the tall windows during the day. It was now replaced by slowly appearing stars, given the later hour. The sound of the trickling waterfall brought a steady peace to the palace, and I was suddenly aware of why the queen often hosted her tea among the flowers.

Tobias shifted uncomfortably before answering. "It's a picnic," he said by way of explanation.

"Well, I can see that much."

He covered his mouth with his fist and cleared his throat. "It's for us."

"For show? The greenhouse seems empty, and it's getting late. Will some of the court be arriving?"

I turned to look at him, the nerves seeming to wash away–being replaced by a contented expression on his face. "There will be no one from the court arriving," he said. "It's just for us."

My heart skipped as we made our way to the blanket, sitting near the waterfall just out of the mist's reach. The intimate space had my mind thinking of what he'd said in the tunnels. He'd found a woman to court–someone who interested him.

I didn't believe he'd risk our ruse, but I wondered if she would experience a picnic like the one before me after I was gone.

Tobias gathered up the basket, producing plates, a loaf of bread that appeared fresh and warm, jams, cheese, wine, and small pastries. He laid the feast out, setting my plate in front of me and filling the flute glass with wine.

"I'm hoping you enjoy picnics?" he said, his voice holding a hint of a question–an edge of nerves that kept fighting to make their appearance.

I looked around the blanket before filling my tableware with at least one of everything as Tobias began doing the same. "I do," I replied, somewhat stunned–mostly confused. "Very much so."

The grapes he had brought could have well been the best grapes I'd ever tasted.

"So," I tried, hoping to broach the subject brought up in the passageways. "The woman you wish to court. Tell me about her."

"What would you like to know?" he asked around a piece of bread with mixed berry jam.

I picked up a piece of cheese, my stomach finally feeling less neglected.

"Tobias," I said, smiling. "We are friends. I'd like to know as much as you're willing to divulge."

Hoping he didn't see the truth of my feelings, I held my pleasant expression. The only thing I could wish for was that whomever this mystery woman was, she would make him happy. That is what mattered most.

"She's beautiful," he said before taking a sip of wine to wash down his food. I watched the glass touch his lips, the way his eyes remained on mine, and something in my chest became frantic–desperate. I kept it carefully locked away despite the way his eyes lit beneath the glittering lights.

I picked up my own glass, glancing toward the waterfall. "I'm certain," I said, smiling behind the flute. "Whomever she is, she will have to compete with your–" I met his gaze, humor dancing in his eyes to match my own. "What did you call it?" I asked. "Ah, yes. Your *compelling* appearance."

My jest dragged a laugh from his chest, deep and rumbling, tugging at the memory of every laugh he'd shared with me before. I knew without a doubt that I'd never be rid of the memory. It had been engraved in my bones–the most pleasant sound.

"Trust me," he said. "It is no contest."

Subtle sadness snuck into my body. I still kept it contained.

"Her beauty is far more than a compelling appearance," he continued. "She is kind, though she keeps to herself. Somewhat reckless in her consumption of cheap beer."

My brows furrowed. "I can't fault her for that."

He laughed again, his head tilting back as he did. "No, you certainly cannot. How many drinks did you have that night, anyway."

"To be honest, I think I lost count."

He took another drink as I watched the column of his throat, the room becoming unbearably hot.

"Well, then," he said, setting his glass back down. "It was lucky I found you when I did. What would have happened if a man had swooped in while you were vulnerable–done something disgraceful."

My head tilted to the side as I fought off a smile. "Like blackmail?"

He was staring at me in earnest now, brown eyes warm and inviting–the flicker of something more than friendship. I couldn't be sure I wasn't imagining it. "I only blackmailed you when you were sober."

"But you did, all the same."

A moment passed between us, charged and lit by a backdrop of fairy lights and stars.

His voice dropped to a whisper as he leaned closer, my own body responding to his nearness. "I have no regrets."

My mouth parted, but the words escaped me. The look in his eyes reminded me of the other day–the very thing that had distracted me during my competition earlier in the day. Somehow, I wasn't thinking of my missed target. I only thought of the warmth radiating off him, the way we were suddenly close enough to share breath–two halves slowly pulled together.

When his mouth hovered just beyond mine with the promise of a kiss, I whispered, "What of the woman you described."

"Luna," he said, his voice rich like the earth. "You are one of the most intelligent women I've met, but in this, you are very stupid."

The ghost of a smile appeared on my lips. "Are you insulting me?" I asked as his hand moved to the side of my face, warm just like everything about him.

"We are friends, are we not?" he whispered. His bottom lip brushed against mine, my breath catching in my throat. "To be very clear, Luna," he said. "I am very interested in *you*."

When he kissed me, the world seemed to fade. Beneath the glittering light of the stars, surrounded by the sounds of water, his lips moved against mine. His fingers tangled in my hair as he deepened the kiss, drawing me closer.

My worries and fears disappeared as I lost myself in the prince, an unlikely pair, the archer and the prince–

But a pair all the same.

Fourteen

"How would you like to use the tunnels once more?"

I laughed, my hand held firmly as we walked toward the door through which we had entered the greenhouse. "I say that sounds like a lovely, adventurous idea."

Tobias conjured another ball of light, illuminating the darkness as we walked through the mysterious passageways behind the castle walls.

"Why were these formed, to begin with?" I asked, running my fingertips along the cool stone.

Tobias glanced sideways, his boots kicking up a small amount of dust from the floors. "Centuries ago, they were used for royals as a precaution. They were built in case of an attack on the royal bloodline. The king's family could move through the palace and find an escape route should the worst happen."

I blinked, suddenly aware of the history etched into the foundation of the palace. "Has anything like that ever occurred?"

"Not in recent history. Edessa hasn't been at war for a long time. The closest thing we've had was the attempted poisoning the spring before last. That still remains somewhat of a mystery." He paused, mulling over his words. "I suppose the situation with your father counts as well."

I nodded in understanding as we walked side by side, the ball of light highlighting the lips that I'd kissed in the greenhouse.

"The woman you intend to court–" I began, realizing he never quite said the words, though I had my suspicions. He had been clear enough, but I simply couldn't help myself.

Tobias stopped, turning to face me. His somewhat exasperated expression was contradicted by the smile remaining on his face. "Are you really asking me this question?"

"Is it Calliope? I know she was a top contender." I rolled my tongue along my cheek, fighting the smile dancing at the corners of my mouth.

"You insufferable woman," he said, though there was no malice in the claim. "Have I not kissed you nearly enough?"

"Not quite."

He leaned down, his finger tilting my chin up as his lips brushed mine, gentle at first but hungrier when a soft noise escaped my lips.

I stepped forward, melting into him, when the sound of glass skidding across the floor drew my attention, causing us to break apart.

"Strange," I said, looking at the vile so similar to the one we'd seen at the entrance to the greenhouse. I knelt down to pick up the container. When my fingers brushed the glass, I noted that it was extremely hot. My hand shot back.

"What is it?" Tobias asked, concerned.

"It's scalding," I said, looking up from my crouch on the ground.

Footsteps sounded in the hall, some distance away from us.

"Get behind me." Tobias reached at his belt beneath his jacket, pulling a dagger that had been sheathed there.

"Do you always carry that?" I asked, my heart racing. Every sound in the tunnels seemed sharper–tainted with worry and fear.

"As a prince? Yes."

"I don't have my bow." My voice was breathless as the footsteps drew nearer.

Tobias reached down into his boot, procuring another knife, though smaller. He handed it to me, keeping his fist wrapped around mine when the hilt was in my hand.

"If anything happens," he said. "Do not hesitate to use this. There shouldn't be anyone in the tunnels."

I gripped the knife tighter as the sound approached. From the left hallway came a man–old and unfamiliar–dressed in a threadbare robe with his hood drawn over his head, casting most of his face in shadow, though I could see enough to view the wrinkles and sagging skin. Even if I hadn't, his hands were a dead giveaway.

"Who are you?" Tobias asked, his voice taking on an authoritative tone–a king in the making, I thought.

After drawing his hood down to reveal the patch of white wispy hair on his head, the old man smiled. His yellow teeth stood crooked in his mouth–some missing entirely.

"Prince Cranefield," he said, his voice sending ice through my veins. "How is your family?"

Something was very wrong.

The man reached into his cloak, collecting something from within and tossing it on the floor. Thick smoke emanated from the broken vial, making the air smell sweet and burn hot.

I watched as Tobias swayed on his feet, the aroma going straight to my head. I stepped forward, the fog overtaking my mind–making me feel dizzy.

"It will only last a moment, dear," the old man crooned. "I'm afraid that dose won't be able to take the both of you, but it will certainly subdue *him* enough for the opportunity."

I stepped forward again as Tobias leaned against the wall, struggling to stay upright.

"Who are you?" I asked, my voice coming out as a rasp.

"An old potions master who wishes to see the kingdom in other hands. If you'd allow me to explain, I think you would agree. The Cranefields have kept Edessa war-free for a century. It's time that changed." His smile widened behind the slowly fading smoke–the same smoke that was taking my consciousness with it. "I'm afraid your father agreed–once given a potion to sway his thinking."

I didn't hesitate.

Gripping the knife, I drove it forward into the man's thigh, a scream pulling from his lips.

The last thing I remember before it all went dark were Tobias's footsteps rushing forward and the realization that I had gleaned an important piece of some puzzle I had been trying to solve.

And I wasn't even wearing my trousers.

FIFTEEN

Sunlight spilled gently through the window when I woke, making me–just briefly–believe I had been waking in Fairvein.

It wasn't until I noted the palace walls around me that I realized my mistake.

It was the same guest room I'd stayed in two weeks ago–the morning of my arrangement with the prince.

"You're awake." Tobias rose from a chair in the corner, quickly finding his way to the bed and sitting by my side. His rolled-up sleeves and half-untucked shirt, as well as the blanket hanging over the chair near the bed, let me know where he had spent his night.

My limbs felt heavy–my brain still struggling to catch up with my surroundings, but the memories began returning like a flood. It was so much I had to be careful not to be washed away in them.

I remembered the man who called himself a potions master, the tunnels, the dagger in my hand and the way it had felt when it dug into his leg. The memory of the sensation made me queasy. At least with an arrow, you never had to feel anything beyond the wind ripping it away from your bow.

I sat up, trying to dispel the nausea. "Where is–" I could hardly finish my sentence, my eyes wild when they turned to Tobias. "The man. Is he gone? What happened?"

"He's gone, and Nessanine is waiting to speak to you when we are done." I noted the healing cut across his brow and lifted my fingers to touch his skin–be sure he was real. Tobias flinched when I did, and I quickly pulled away.

"Sorry," I muttered.

"That potion–no poison–he used was quite strong, Luna. You've been asleep for two days." His hand came to rest over mine, warm and gentle, just as I remembered. "He–" His brows furrowed, mind searching for the words. "That man is in the dungeons beneath the palace awaiting questioning. He revealed some information that we cannot ignore."

I'm afraid your father agreed–once given the potion to sway his thinking.

"My father–" I started, my chest feeling as if it would cleave in two.

Tobias shook his head, sorrow apparent in the muscles of his face. "I am so sorry, Luna."

I nodded, allowing the silence to wrap around us like a blanket. Grief would come–this I knew. As I sat on the bed in Prince Cranefield's presence, I couldn't help but ponder all the moments I had felt I never truly knew my father–how it wasn't true.

"We suspect there may be others," Tobias finally continued. "This could possibly be linked to what occurred in Fairvein. We are not sure yet."

"But why would he hide in the palace walls? And if he were hiding there, what was stopping him from doing it himself."

A crease formed between his brow–stress etched into his skin. "We aren't entirely sure, though we found no other signs of him living there. The entrances to the tunnels from outside–the ones that used to be used in case of a needed escape have been sealed off. He could have gotten in at any time. They are old—the entrances grown over and difficult to open, but not impossible." He cleared his throat. "Clearly."

I glanced out the tall windows, the evergreens dotted with remaining shades of orange and gold—autumn stretching all the way to the Agmund mountains. It was strange to think that in a kingdom as peaceful as Edessa, there may be something nefarious lying in wait. How anyone could *desire* war struck me as odd, but magic existed. Its roots stretched throughout the entire continent, even lingering beneath the sea until they reached the far corners of the country. Corners like the safe pocket of Fairvein.

The unfortunate thing about magic was that it could drive anyone to madness—including old men who found their way into the palace.

"I must say," Tobias began, his tone turning lighter. "I felt incredibly safe with you around. You did not hesitate in stabbing the man."

A small laugh left my lips, the only way to cope with the situation. "Brutal," I said. "I didn't know I had it in me."

"You would make a superb guard." He paused, a sad smile tugging at the corners of his mouth. "If that is what you still want, that is."

I leaned back against the headboard, releasing a breath. "I'm not sure it is anymore," I admitted. "I'm assuming with my two-day absence, I was withdrawn from the competition. Even so, I can't bring myself to care as much—not after what we went through." Pain struck my chest at the thought of my father—at the puzzle solved within the palace walls. "I guess my desire to be on the guard came from two places," I started. "One, I longed to understand what my father had done. Discover what had gone wrong. And it seems I've done that." My eyes met his—rapt with attention. "Two, it felt like the only thing I'd ever been good at—archery. The guard seemed like a logical choice."

Tobias's thumb stroked the top of my hand, reminding me he was still holding it—refusing to drop it no matter what.

"You're quite good at protecting royalty," he admitted. "It has its uses. The guard, for instance," he said, shifting slightly. "But it is also a good quality to have no matter what."

I allowed the silence to stretch between us, sensing he had more to say.

"I'd like to court you, Luna Ellsworth. If you'd allow me."

A fluttering feeling danced in my stomach. "But, Prince Cranefield," I said, fighting the smile threatening to break free. "We are already engaged."

"And so we are." His smile stretched wide, speaking of a place that could finally feel like home. "We will have to tell my mother the truth, at the very least."

My brow furrowed. "Will she be upset?"

He chuckled, leaning forward as his voice lowered. "Absolutely furious, but don't worry. Her love is stronger than her anger. She will recover."

I laughed then, allowing the joy to seep into the sorrow—ease the pain of the last few days.

"I suppose I could afford a few more nights at the inn, though I should be careful of their drink. It is quite strong, you know."

Tobias wrapped his hand around the back of my neck, pulling me in to place a kiss on my forehead. "Ridiculous," he said. "You're welcome to stay in the palace as long as you like."

"Oh, good. It would be an insult if you were to court a woman and leave her at a dusty old inn."

"An insult indeed," he mused. "But we are friends, are we not?"

Epilogue

"You really read the book I sent you?" I asked, pulling Tobias through the cobbled street.

Spring began making its exit as the summer season rolled in, promising a bright tourist season for Farivein. After the island's feature in the queen's brochure, there'd been an uptick in summer guests. It bode well for the pockets of the locals–though I don't think they cared much for that. The people of Fairvein were far more concerned with parties and gossip.

I couldn't blame them. Especially when I had left for an archery competition last fall and returned with a prince on my arm.

It made for gossip even I wouldn't have been able to resist.

"Yes, I did," Tobias answered through a laugh. "But Luna," he said, stopping me in my tracks. "The content was quite–scandalous."

"Oh please," I waved a hand, brushing off his concern. "Nothing you haven't participated in before. Scandalous reading is the joy of book club. Tea and Tomes could be nothing less."

We continued walking, the evening air bringing a gentle breeze–promising the warmth of summer.

"And Maxwell allows these discussions in his shop?"

"He not only allows it, Tobias Cranefield," I scolded. "He recommends half the reading."

The door to Maxwell's shop opened before we had the chance to do it ourselves. Isla stood with a plate in her hand, a wide smile plastered to her pale, freckled face.

"I made scones!" she said. I didn't miss the way she fought the urge to gawk at the prince. If Isla was anything, she was easy to read. The woman wore her heart on her sleeve. In fact, she often chose to project her feelings into the sky—calling the attention of everyone on the island.

"Whose recipe?" I asked, smiling warmly in greeting.

She frowned. "That's insulting, Luna. How long have you been purchasing tea from my shop? I have every right to serve you something disgusting after what you just said."

Sylvia huffed a laugh from where she was seated in a comfortable chair, surrounded by the usual attendees. "If those scones are not Cyris's recipe, then you are certainly serving something disgusting."

"Mind your tongue," Isla scolded, turning to point a finger in the girl's direction. "I will have you fired."

"Sylvia," Clementine chimed in from her own seat, her extravagant gown decorated with embroidered cherries. "Are you old enough to attend book club?"

"I turned eighteen last fall."

Clementine giggled, looking toward her friend, the insulted tea shop owner who took her plate of scones and set them on the check-out counter. Maxwell quickly scooped one up, taking a large bite and muttering his thanks—a clear attempt at kindness.

"We're extremely pleased to have you, Prince Cranefield," Clementine continued. "I took it upon myself to consider this gathering to be an engagement celebration. I've brought two bottles of wine. One to celebrate Luna and the prince, and one for Isla and Cyris."

I looked at Isla, her cheeks tinted pink at the acknowledgment.

I found myself running my thumb along my ring, feeling the warm metal where it encircled my finger. Tobias quickly noticed and wove his fingers through mine.

"A celebration," he said. "What a wonderful idea."

Sylvia looked up from her chair. "We are here to discuss the book," she said, her lips turned downward.

"Enjoy this one, did you?" Birdie chimed in as she appeared from Maxwell's office in the back.

The room quickly erupted with lively discussions of *The Warlock's Bride*, wrapping the bookstore in a feeling of warmth.

"You're smiling," Tobias observed from his spot next to me.

"How could you not?"

He squeezed my hand gently. "I'm glad we chose to move into the castle on the island. I see why you kept coming back here."

I smiled wider, watching as Sylvia and Clementine entered a heated argument surrounding the love triangle in the novel we read this week. "What makes you say that?"

"I can't quite put my finger on it," he said. "Save for the fact that I could see this island beginning to feel like home."

I leaned my head against his shoulder, taking in the scene before us, unable to shake the thought that Tobias Cranefield was completely right. Fairvein was perfect. Even more so with him in it.

It was home.

Acknowledgements

So many people to thank and so little time!

First, I'd like to thank Monroe for joining me in the coolest world ever created. I love being able to explore all of these characters with you while laughing and imagining the craziest scenarios. I wouldn't be half the author I am without you and your encouragement. I would also be a crappy human being without being made fun of for literally every tiny mistake or idea, and I have you to thank for that.

Also, I hope your candied oranges always look like they were made by a literal rock.

Second, I would like to thank Reanna for your editing and friendship. I'm sorry I write tombs instead of tomes so often. I'm also sorry that I don't know how to use a comma. You're a saint for dealing with my shit.

This book would not exist without my dad. Thank you for teaching me about archery, for taking me bow hunting, and for being such a great Pawpaw. I love you.

As always, I have to thank my husband for being my number one sugar daddy. Thank you for supporting my author career and teaching me what it means to truly love. My books would not be romantic in the slightest without you.

Finally, I'd like to thank all of the readers who continue to come back to Fairvein with us. We couldn't be more thankful for your presence and support, and I hope that I'm able to do all your favorite characters justice.

ABOUT THE AUTHOR

Emma Steinbrecher typically writes New Adult Fantasy as well as New Adult Romantic Comedy under the pen name Emmie J. Holland.

She lives in Ohio with her two dogs, her son, and her husband.

When she's not writing, she enjoys hiking, learning new hobbies, and reading.

If you're anxious to read any of her other works, here is a list of the books.

A Clan of Wolves Duology

A Clan of Wolves by Emma Steinbrecher (Book 1)

A House of Witches by Emma Steinbrecher (Book 2)

The Death Hunting Trilogy

The Death Hunting by Emma Steinbrecher (Book 1)

The Raidan Awakening by Emma Steinbrecher (Book 2)

The Light Conquering by Emma Steinbrecher (Book 3)

Emmie J. Holland

The Unbelievable Misadventures of Olive Finch by Emmie J. Holland

Pride, Pancakes, & Paris by Emmie J. Holland

The Fairvein Series

Want to read the whole series?

1. *Clementine's Parlor of the Extraordinary and Curious* by Monroe A Wildrose

2. *The Queen's Guide to Teapots and Pastries* by Emma Steinbrecher

3. *Tailor Troubles* by Monroe A Wildrose

4. *The Archer and The Prince* by Emma Steinbrecher

And more to come!